CHAPTER 1

One day Miss Rogers danced into the classroom, smiling the rare smile of a teacher who has just had a cup of strong coffee and a good idea.

'Pay attention,' she cried to her class. 'Particularly you, Formby Mackinaw! I have a new project for you all . . . something that will improve your writing and spelling, and do good to others at the same time.'

Formby Mackinaw groaned loudly.

'Let's have grinning, not groaning!' shouted Miss Rogers. 'Now, is everyone listening?'

All the goody-goodies in the class began grinning and listening hard.

'Our school library money has been spent,' cried Miss Rogers. 'We just *had* to have a new coffee machine for the teachers' staffroom, but buying that coffee machine does mean we can't afford new library books for the next six months. Yet we *need* new books. We *must* have new books. What on earth are we going to do?'

'Close the school!' muttered Formby Mackinaw. Miss Rogers ignored this brilliant idea.

'We'll write the books *ourselves*,' she cried. 'Everyone in this class is going to write at least one new book. Then we will put the best of them in the library. How about that?'

'Great idea, Miss Rogers,' called the goody-goodies, knowing how all teachers love to be praised.

'Jot down any thoughts that come to you over the next day or two,' said Miss Rogers. 'Then we will divide into conference groups, discuss our ideas, and, well, hey-ho for great literature and free library books. Any questions?'

Formby put up his hand.

'Well, Formby?' asked Miss Rogers, narrowing her eyes.

'What if all the ideas we get are *rude* ones?' asked Formby.

'Rude books are definitely not allowed in the school library,' said Miss Rogers severely. 'Parents would want to borrow them, and they would never be on the shelves. Now, if I let you out of school ten minutes early, do you all promise . . . absolutely, utterly, *faithfully* promise . . . to spend your extra ten minutes of free time thinking up good ideas for school library books?'

'Yes, Miss Rogers,' shouted the class, including Formby Mackinaw. If writing books meant getting out of school ten minutes early, then he would certainly promise to write some.

'Good boy, Formby,' said Miss Rogers, smiling at him. 'I know I can trust you. Class dismissed.'

Formby was delighted. An extra ten minutes meant that he could get through the park without fear of meeting Aspen Twinkler, a great big bullying boy with a small brain but bony elbows. Aspen was jealous of Formby's skill at video games, and he always took over Formby's favourite game at the video arcade. Even if Formby was there first, Aspen would elbow him away, using elbows as sharp as space swords. Not only that, Aspen would some-times ambush Formby in the park and rub his hair the wrong way. Getting out of class ten minutes early gave Formby a chance to race through the park and to have two or three games at the video arcade before Aspen Twinkler arrived there.

'Waste my time thinking of a story as I walk home?' muttered Formby, as he jogged out of the school yard and into the park. 'Old Rogers must be mad.'

And yet, as he thought this, a name came into his mind.

Squidgy Moot!

It was like being stung by a wasp.

Formby came to a standstill within sight of the cactus house. At first he thought he was going to sneeze, for he often had hay fever when it was springtime and there was a lot of pollen floating around the park. However, whatever it was that was stirring in his head seemed even more serious than sneezing.

'Squidgy Moot!' he exclaimed aloud, then added in much puzzled voice, 'Squidgy Moot?'

He shrugged.

Whatever made me think of a name like that? he wondered. And he began running through the park anxious to reach the video arcade and to blast hundreds of computer aliens before Aspen Twinkler arrived, bringing his elbows with him.

Formby longed for the day when his father, who had installed an extremely clever computer in the office at home, would allow his only son to sit on the office whirl-around chair and play computer games to his utter heart's content.

CHAPTER 2

As he jogged past the cactus house, Formby suddenly heard the sound of wicked chuckling. He looked sideways. Someone was loping beside him ... someone strange and shadowy with hair like thick black fur ... someone wearing a black shirt, blue baggy trousers and long, laced-up Doc Martens boots. The stranger smiled a sinister smile when he saw that Formby had noticed him. He had teeth like white needles.

Of course, Formby knew he should not talk to needle-toothed strangers. Yet he had the ghostly feeling that he already knew this stranger quite well.

'What do *you* want?' Formby cried.

The toothy one grinned even harder. He curled his fingers into the shape of binoculars, clapped them to his eyes and peered at Formby.

'Hey whacko!' he cried. 'You look to me like someone who is planning to write a *book*.'

'No way!' Formby exclaimed.

'You *have* to,' cried the toothy one. 'Someone has to write my story, and I have chosen you. Your book will be placed on the library shelves. People will read of my wicked doings and gasp with horror. Why, my wickedness might even be turned into a film or a computer game.'

Formby came to a standstill.

'Who *are* you?' he asked. 'What's your name?'

'My name is Moot,' said the sharp-toothed one. 'Squidgy Moot! I suddenly found myself loping along through the wide world, planning all sorts of wickedness as I loped. Hey whacko! I thought. Some good writer has invented me. Shakespeare, probably! Immediately I decided to become a rich villain. No goody-goody heroes for me. But somehow I can't actually *do* my wicked doings until someone writes them down. So start writing!'

'Get someone else to write them,' said Formby. 'I'm not a writer. I play video games.'

'But everyone else in your class is a goody-goody,' whined the sharp-toothed one. 'They won't want to write about wickedness. No! *You* thought me up, *you* invented my name, so now *you* have to do what I tell you to do. Hurry home at once, find that pen that writes in seven colours and the De Luxe Data notebook that your Uncle Aidan gave you last Christmas. Then, hey whacko! Scribble down a lot of adventures – I don't mind how *wicked* you make me – and a lot of money for me at the end of the story. That's what "happily ever after" means.'

'Get lost!' cried Formby. Yet, as he spoke, his head began whirling with words. He grew dizzy, sneezed and staggered around. It was much worse than hay fever.

Somehow, Formby knew that the only way to get those whirling words out of his head would be to *write* them out.

Squidgy Moot gave a triumphant laugh.

'Hey whacko!' he cried yet again, and disappeared, leaving Formby in a terrible state, for he felt as if he had a mad firework shooting backwards and forwards in his head, exploding every time it bounced off the inside of his skull. He fully expected coloured sparks to spray out of his ears.

The sooner I write this story the sooner I can get back to video games, he thought, and made desperately for home.

CHAPTER 3

As Formby burst into the living room and slung his
backpack in the corner, his mother glanced up from
a magazine filled with tales of the royal family.

'Had a nice day, dear?' she asked.

'I have to write a story about a villain called
Squidgy Moot,' groaned Formby. 'A whole story!
A real book! And when I've finished it, it's going to
be shelved in the school library, just like a proper,
printed, published one,' he couldn't help boasting.

Formby's little sister, Minnie, was in the kitchen,
pouring herself a glass of milk and listening in to
other people's business – something she was always
doing.

'I'll help you,' she cried eagerly. 'I know a lot about Squidgy Moot.'

'You don't,' said Formby, scornfully. 'I've only just invented him.'

'I do so,' said Minnie, and stuck out her tongue, all slimy, pale and dripping with milk. 'Anyhow, Squidgy Moot's nothing much. He has a little sister called Nina Moot who is much cleverer than he is.'

'He does *not*,' shouted Formby. 'He's too wicked to bother with sisters. I'm the *author*, which means I'm the boss, and I say there are no sisters in my story. It's a horror story and it's not going to be written in sissy, soppy, little-kid felt tips! I'm going to write it in my own blood.'

'Liar! Liar! Your pants are on fire!' yelled Minnie, scornfully. 'I'll bet you're going to use that pen that writes in seven colours. What if you get hay fever and start sneezing? Oh, Foooormby, let me help you.'

'No!' shouted Formby. He raced into his room, slammed the door and pushed a chair against it. Then he ran to the desk by his bookcase and quickly found the special notebook his uncle had given him last Christmas. It had a shiny black cover with the words 'De Luxe Data Book' printed on it. Inside it had a calendar for the year before last, a list of international telephone dialling codes, and a page telling you the times in different parts of the world. Formby drew out his special seven-colour pen, like a video-game warrior drawing his zoot gun, and clicked it to blood red.

Good writers have to put up with a lot of jealousy, he thought. Particularly from little sisters! Now, let me see! How will I begin?

His frowning face brightened. I know. I'll write the first line, and if I make it very exciting maybe it'll sweep me on to the second line. Yes, that's it! I'll make the first line so exciting that anyone reading it will just *have* to go on and read the second line, and anyone who reads the second line will just *have* to read the third, and so on. So my story will begin on the blackest night that ever was.

And he began writing.

CHAPTER 4

It was the blackest night that ever was. Lightning stabbed down into the city. Thunder rattled the roofs. In the city square the clock was striking the hour of doom. The famous villain Squidgy Moot came sliding into the square like an oily shadow, making for the house of Professor Mockery, the amazing scientist. Lightning flashed. There in front of him, Squidgy Moot saw the face of a furious piranha. He leaped back in alarm. But the next flash showed him it was only his own picture grinning at him from a police poster pasted on the wall of a nearby post office. WANTED FOR WICKEDNESS said the big print under the picture. Squidgy Moot waited until the lightning flashed a third time, and then grinned back at it.

'Wanted? I should think I am,' he muttered proudly. 'As villains go I'm remarkably handsome.'

Then he oiled his way onward, for Squidgy Moot was not sliding past the post office, on the blackest night that ever was, simply to post a few letters. He was planning a sensational robbery.

Only last year Professor Mockery, who lived next door to the post office, had won the Nobel Prize for Computer Games. And only the day before, a headline in the paper had caught Squidgy Moot's eye. COUNT ASPIO RETURNS! PROFESSOR MOCKERY INVENTS SENSATIONAL NEW VIDEO GAME! Squidgy was delighted. It seemed you slid a CD-ROM into your computer (if you didn't have a computer you used the one at the nearest library), and then slipped on a special helmet that plugged in right next to the disk drive. Instantly, amazing adventures leaped on to the screen, then out of the screen, and within a minute you were engulfed by adventures that seemed utterly real – more than real – realer than real. The moment he read about this new realer-than-real computer game, Squidgy Moot knew he just had to have it. So, on this dark night of storm and shadow, he was planning to break into the Mockery mansion, find both the disk and the helmet, steal them and carry them home to his own computer (which was connected to the Internet, a wonderful web of computers, stretching every-whichever-way around the world). Once he had that disk and the helmet, Squidgy would be able to play incredible computer games all afternoon.

Professor Mockery lived with his sister, the famous artist Elsivera Mockery, in the strangest house in the square. It was five-storeys high and covered from top to bottom with illustrations of weird planets and the aliens who lived on them, all painted by Elsivera Mockery herself. There were eagle men, wolf women and serpents with wings. There were cat people from the planet Purr-Purr, and a sludge dragon from Pong the sewerage planet. Over the front door was the picture of a ferocious alien warrior with tusks, curling horns, hairy ears and sharp, bony elbows. This hideous alien was no stranger to Squidgy Moot. He immediately recognized one of Professor Mockery's famous inventions . . . Count Aspio, the wickedest, ugliest, most bullying warrior in the computer-game universe. There he was, larger than life and sticking out his elbows like swords. Indeed the outside of the Mockery house looked like a sort of computer game itself. Computer-game freaks and tourists came from all over the world to take photographs of it. Now, as lightning flashed, the painted figures seemed to writhe, to roll their eyes and to snap their teeth with an eerie trembling life that would have terrified anyone except a good computer-game player. Count Aspio seemed to grimace, gnash his tusks and joggle his sharp elbows at Squidgy Moot.

But Squidgy simply sneered. 'He's nothing but an illustration,' he muttered to himself. 'I'm interested in wickedness not art. Anyhow, I'm not scared of bullies.'

He slid, in his oily way, into the shadows of the ivy that tangled around the doorway, then touched the huge, iron door handle, which was almost as big as his head. A lot of automatic lights cleverly switched themselves on, running pale fingers across his wicked face. Squidgy gave his wide, flickering needle-filled smile. Green eyes flashing, he pulled out a little black box which he pointed at the lock. This was an 'Open Sesame' door opener, a special present he had found in the bottom of his stocking two Christmases ago. He pressed a button. ZZZZT! Out shot an unlocking ray straight into the keyhole, which immediately glowed like hot gold. The door groaned, trying to hold itself shut, but all in vain. KERBLAM! The locks couldn't help themselves. They just had to explode. The door sprang open.

'Aha!' cried Squidgy Moot, dancing with joy. 'By tomorrow I will be in the headlines of every newspaper in the world. Tomorrow I will be wearing Professor Mockery's computer helmet. Tomorrow I will be playing Professor Mockery's new realer-than-real computer game on my own computer. Hey whacko!'

He switched on a special burglar's torch, and dived into the blackness beyond the doorway. The torchlight slid nervously across a notice hanging on the door of the Mockery elevator. 'Lift out of order!' it said. 'Spies and burglars please climb the internut to the floor you require.' The torchlight revealed something astonishing. There were no stairs in the Mockery house. Instead, a huge nut tree grew from the bottom floor through what would have been called a stairwell in any other house. Staring up into the tangle of branches, Squidgy Moot made out ladders nailed from top to bottom of the massive tree trunk. Certain branches led directly to doors set in the inner wall.

'I suppose they think we burglars are too weak to climb an internut,' muttered Squidgy. 'I'll soon show them.' He swarmed up the first ladder, and then began scrambling, softly at first, from branch to branch, smiling as he climbed.

One thing was certain — no shy, retiring Nobel Prizewinner should ever have to face up to a smile like Squidgy Moot's.

CHAPTER 5

Formby sat back and looked at what he had written. He was amazed at how good it was. Of course he *had* met Squidgy Moot before he actually wrote a single word on his De Luxe Data pages, but he had totally invented Professor Mockery, the illustrated Mockery house, and the mysterious science-fiction artist Elsivera all by himself. He felt particularly proud of the internut, growing up through the house and putting out branches at each floor.

'I've made a pun. Only good writers think of things like that,' he muttered to himself. 'It just shows what the right first line can lead to.' He particularly enjoyed the way he was somehow making secret fun of Aspen Twinkler, by turning him into the ugly illustration of Count Aspio on the wall of the Mockery house.

Formby then began to draw his own picture of Count Aspio. His pen scribbled and dived and darted. After he stopped scribbling, he sat staring at his illustrations. They were good, but somehow not good enough. Formby frowned at them, then shrugged his shoulders. 'Better than nothing,' he told himself. 'And anyway I am a writer not an illustrator.'

His mother came marching in without knocking – a bad habit of hers. She saw his pictures before he could hide them.

'Don't you have any homework to do?' she asked.

'This *is* homework,' said Formby. 'I told you that we had to write a book for the school library.' He could see Minnie watching from the doorway. 'Don't watch me,' he shouted. 'Authors hate to be watched.'

'I could give you good ideas,' Minnie shouted back.

'I've got millions of good ideas,' cried Formby. 'I don't need yours. I've done the first chapter and I'm just going to begin on chapter two.'

'Well, it's time for dinner,' said Formby's mother. 'Not that I want to interrupt your homework, but I'm about to unwrap the fish and chips.'

Formby found he was starving. It seemed there

was nothing like writing a story of mystery and danger to whip up a great appetite. He leaped to his feet and was about to charge out of the room, leaving the De Luxe Data Book open on his desk, when he realized that his mother might come in on some picking-up-and-folding expedition and read everything he'd written before it was ready to be read. Placing his precious story tenderly in an old shoe box, he quickly tied string around it using a complicated knot called a slingstone hitch.

An interknot! he thought, laughing at his own cleverness as he looped the ends of the string back into the knot so that anyone wanting to untie it wouldn't know where to begin.

Then he wrote the words 'PRIVATE! KEEP OUT!' on the box, thrust it into the back of the wardrobe where it would be protected by his smelly gym shoes, and went down to dinner, whistling cheerfully.

After dinner he and Minnie watched television, crying 'Yuck! Yuck!' and covering their eyes whenever people kissed, until their parents, who secretly enjoyed the kissing, shouted that television was bad for them, and drove them both to bed.

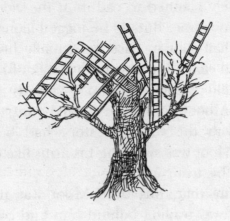

CHAPTER 6

After school the following day, as Formby came home through the park, someone elbowed him in the side, almost knocking him over. Of course it was Aspen Twinkler. Formby knew he was going to be slightly bullied, but he remembered writing about hideous Count Aspio and for some strange reason this comforted him. It was as if he knew a mocking secret about Aspen that Aspen had no possible way of knowing about himself.

'Are you going to the video arcade, Mac?' Aspen cried. 'Make the most of it, because I've got to go home early today.' Then he jabbed Formby again, ruffled his hair and ran on by.

That wasn't much, thought Formby bravely, and immediately planned to call in at the video arcade on the way home. But, as he jogged along (holding his nose half shut in case he actually breathed in pollen and came down with an attack of hay fever), who should come bounding towards him, but Squidgy Moot. Formby expected him to be delighted with the way the story had begun, but Squidgy Moot was swinging his arms like clubs and snapping his teeth with fury.

Not only that, this time Moot was not alone. Someone was trailing behind him and copying his gestures . . . swinging arms like smaller clubs and snapping teeth with a smaller but even-fiercer fury. Formby narrowed his eyes trying to work out who it might be, but Squidgy Moot quickly took all Formby's attention, leaping and dancing in front of him and spreading out his arms so that Formby found it hard to see past him.

'How dare you?' Squidgy Moot was crying. 'How dare you?'

'How dare you yell "How dare you!" at me?' Formby shouted back. 'I've written you down, haven't I? I've described your teeth like white needles. I've arranged it so that you are in the act of breaking into a famous scientist's laboratory. You're going to steal his realer-than-real computer game. Isn't that enough for a kick-off?'

'Listen, you fool!' hissed Squidgy Moot. 'What

do you suppose I found at the top of that nut tree
. . . you do remember that *internut*, I suppose? The
one with branches connecting the bottom to the top
of the Mockery house? Ha! Ha! Very funny!'

'I *invented* those branches,' said Formby proudly.

'And I've had to *climb* them. But never mind that
now!' said Squidgy Moot. 'The point is: what did I
find when I got to the top?'

'What?' asked Formby.

'Something terrible! Something no writer – no
good writer, that is – should ever allow. Something
more loathsome than the Sludge Dragon of Pong
the sewerage planet.'

'What?' repeated Formby.

'My little sister!' screamed Squidgy Moot. 'My
little sister was up there waiting for me. It's bad
enough to have little sisters trailing along after you
when you are trying to do something wicked, but
it's a thousand times worse when a little sister gets
there first. Look at her grinning!'

And sure enough there, about seven steps behind
him, was a little sister, smaller than Squidgy Moot,
but every bit as wicked. In fact, being smaller somehow made the wickedness fiercer – more concen-
trated.

'I want to be a villain too,' she cried. 'Mum says
I'm *allowed* to.'

Squidgy snapped his teeth, and growled like a
mad bear.

'Get away!' he snarled at her. 'I don't want you hanging around me. Go and climb into some picture book! Have a game of lambie-wammies or bunny-wunnies, or play dolls, or go and talk to little, useless villains your own age.'

The little sister was square shaped with wild, tangled hair. She had points like ballpoint pens on the end of her shoes. Her teeth were just as white as Squidgy's, though not quite as long. They looked more like pins than needles.

'I'm about to steal a realer-than-real computer game in this boy's story,' Squidgy went on, 'and I've got to do it in some amazingly clever way, or the story will fall to bits.' He looked at Formby.

'Why did you write *her* into the story?' he said.

'I *didn't*!' cried Formby. 'I didn't even know you *had* a sister. Minnie – that is someone I know, someone little and stupid – did say you had a sister, but I didn't believe her. I've never heard of villains having little sisters.'

'Well, how did she get into the story if you didn't write her in?' asked Squidgy Moot. 'Write her *out* of it at once.'

At these words the little sister hurled herself on Squidgy.

'I'll bite you if you make him write me out! I'll tell Mum!'

Squidgy Moot and his little sister began rolling

over and over, shouting and snapping at one another.

Filled with alarm, Formby ran all the way home, leaving the yowling Moots behind him.

What's going on? he thought. I certainly didn't write anything about any little sister in *my* story. What's happened to it while I've been forced to spend valuable time at school against my will?

CHAPTER 7

Formby burst into the kitchen where his mother was having a quiet cup of tea while reading a novel about love in Hollywood. She glanced up guiltily as he stamped through the room, for she had been planning to tell her family that she had been slaving all afternoon, cleaning burnt cheese out of the oven.

'Have you had a nice day, dear?' she asked in her most motherly voice. 'Do you want a cookie? Minnie ran home extra-quickly today and has had two cookies already.' But Formby was racing down the hall to his room. Holding his breath he opened his wardrobe and reached past his smelly gym shoes to find the box with his notebook in it. There it was, tied up, just as he had left it. Or so it *seemed*!

Yet, as he stared at the box, Formby noticed one significant detail. The interknot holding the ends of string together was not the elegant slingstone hitch *he* had tied, but more like a nest of tangled tiger worms.

It was the work of a moment – well, to be strictly honest it was the work of several moments, say about ten moments or even fifteen – to unknot this worm-ish knot and to take out the De Luxe Data Book. Horrakapotchkin! Pages five, six and seven were now filled with someone else's handwriting – and with pictures as well. His story had been corrupted!

Of course, Formby knew just who to blame. Minnie! Minnie must have taken a short cut through her friend Sandra's backyard. Then (pausing only to grab two cookies) she had searched his room, found his story, *and she must have written a new chapter*.

As Formby began reading this mysterious new chapter, his mouth fell open and he turned pale with dismay and indignation. And as he read, he felt Squidgy Moot reading over his shoulder. When they gasped in horror, they gasped in horror together.

This was what they were reading.

CHAPTER 8

Squidgy Moot climbed from branch to branch, ignoring all doors until he came to the top one. Then he hung there, panting so hard he sounded like a walrus who has just turned seventeen cartwheels around the edge of an iceberg. Then he turned the door handle quietly and carefully. Alas! The door was tightly locked on the inside.

'Hey whacko! The secret laboratory must be behind this door,' thought Squidgy Moot. 'I knew it would be at the top of the house.' Out with his 'Open Sesame' door opener! Bing! Bing! The keyhole glowed. The locks gave way. The door sighed and opened, and Squidgy Moot, seizing the

branch above him, swung into the room beyond.

What a shock for a hard-working villain! The air was filled with the scent of old socks and the sound of growling tigers. Squidgy Moot was terrified.

'Terrified?' shouted Squidgy Moot in Formby's ear. 'Me? Me terrified? No way!'

'I keep telling you – I didn't write any of this!' shouted Formby, tired of his complaints. 'Let's finish reading, and then we'll work out what to do.'

Light from the city came in through a window and showed Squidgy Moot that there wasn't a single electron microscope or particle disintegrator in sight. There, directly in front of him, was a four-poster bed looped with billowing curtains. A sleeping man – a famous scientist judging by his moustache – lay propped up on pillows with his mouth open and his eyes closed. His fine moustache, ragged and grey as rain clouds, whiffled gracefully up and down, for the sleeper was snoring loudly.

On the far side of the bed stood a big wardrobe and, across the room, directly in front of Squidgy, was another door. You could easily tell, just from the look of it, that, once again, the door was tightly locked. Squidgy tiptoed towards it. There seemed to be some sort of printing on the front of this door. He peered at it in the dim light.

MOCKERY STUDIO, the words said, set out in the sort of bright magnetic letters parents stick on fridges to encourage little kids to read. ALL

INTERNATIONAL PIES AND BURGERS
KEEP OUT!!!

'Pies and Burgers?' muttered Squidgy Moot, baffled. *'International Pies and Burgers?'*

Something clicked down by his foot. He picked it up. It was the red letter 'S'. And there beside it was another letter . . . a blue one . . . an 'L'.

Villians are very quick-witted. Squidgy put the magnetic S in front of the word 'PIES' and the 'L' in the middle of 'BURGERS'.

SPIES AND BURGLERS

'Wrong spelling!' shouted Formby triumphantly. ' "Burglars" is spelt with an "a" at the end, not an "e". Little sisters are dumb.'

'Forget the spelling!' shouted Squidgy Moot in Formby's ear.

'No,' said Formby cunningly. 'If this book has good spelling, Miss Rogers will be sure to put it in the school library.'

'Oh, all right then,' said Squidgy Moot, relaxing and suddenly looking rather pleased at the thought of such fame. They went on reading.

At that moment Squidgy Moot heard a faint rustle behind him and utterly unexpected fingers fell on his arm. He spun round, hissing and snapping his teeth.

There behind him was a girl, snapping back at him and smiling with just as many teeth as Squidgy himself – just as many and just as pointed. Squidgy

Moot turned instantly green with horror. IT WAS HIS LITTLE SISTER, NINA MOOT.

'How did you get here?' he whispered fiercely. 'Why aren't you at home, learning to cook crumbed slugs?'

'I'm allowed to be wicked if I want to,' said Nina. 'Girls are allowed to have careers these days. I've got an "Open Sesame" door opener just as you have, and I want to find the realer-than-real computer game just as much as you do. And, anyhow, I got here first. Ha ha ha ha ha!'

The new chapter ended with a burst of whispery but mocking laughter.

CHAPTER 9

'Minnie!' muttered Formby, staring at his precious De Luxe Data Book, now defaced by someone else's handwriting. 'She's taken a short cut over the back fence of her friend Sandra, she's found my book and written little-sister bits into *my* story. I'll just rip them out.'

He seized the little-sister pages firmly.

'Stop! Stop!' shouted Squidgy Moot. 'Don't tear those pages out, or you'll do terrible damage to us all.' He was looking far more frightencd than you would expect anyone who owned so many sharp teeth to look. And suddenly, there behind him was Nina Moot who must have sneaked in, looking triumphant as little sisters often do when they are successfully spying on an innocent big brother.

'But there are plenty of pages left. I'll write some new adventures,' offered Formby.

Nina snapped her teeth at him.

'You'll be really sorry if you tear me out,' she said, 'because I have been invented with special shoes. See those spikes on the end of my boots? Those spikes are hollow and fire zoot particles. You are going to need boots like mine in a story like yours, and you can't have these boots without me inside them.'

'If you tear those pages out, you'll tear me out too,' said Squidgy Moot, breathing hard in Formby's ear. 'I don't know why, but that's the way it is.'

'All right,' said Formby. 'But I'll have a terrible revenge when I write the next chapter.'

'That's the spirit,' said Squidgy Moot, recovering rapidly and giving a nasty laugh. 'OK! Maybe we can't tear little sisters out of the story once some fool – I name no names, but look in the mirror – has let some *other* little sister write them in, but we *can* rearrange the story so that all little sisters come to a bad end.'

'Don't you dare!' shouted Nina Moot. 'Little sisters are the *best*!'

'Ah ha ha-HA ha!' cried Squidgy Moot. 'That's

frightened her. Get to it, Formby! Write your heart out! Quickly! Quickly!'

Formby snatched up his seven-coloured pen and began writing with desperate speed.

CHAPTER 10

Squidgy Moot stared at his sister in despair. But then his eyes brightened and a look of great cunning passed over his face. He knew Nina had a fatal weakness. She loved it when he let her join in with his games.

'All right!' he whispered. 'Now you're here, you can help me. I'll look through the papers on this table by the bed – where the snoring is much the worst – while you search that wardrobe over there.'

Nina beamed with delight.

'OK,' she said, and made for the wardrobe.

Squidgy Moot shuffled some of the pages on the table by Professor Mockery's bed. Though he was merely pretending to look through them, he couldn't help noticing many little pads of paper, all filled with drawings. Of course he had to keep an eye on Nina (and on Professor Mockery too) but there was something about those drawings that made him pause in the middle of his shuffling. The wild shapes and spirals seemed to mean something – but what could a lot of scribbles possibly mean? He turned the scribbles right and left, then held them out at arm's length, staring at them in an unexpected moment of dreamy wonder.

Meanwhile, Nina had tiptoed to the tall wardrobe and thrown it open. Leaning far into the shadows of the wardrobe she began a scruffling of her own.

Squidgy Moot pulled himself together. His eyes glowed greenly. Shaking his head to jiggle the strange spirals out of his thoughts, he ran on wicked tiptoe behind his little sister. One great push – kerplomp! Nina tumbled deep into the wardrobe. Squidgy clicked the door shut behind her, then hastily swung a heavy chair in front of it. Professor Mockery's snoring was so thunderous that the dragging of a chair could not be heard at all. All the same, Nina dared not give one of her famous eagle shrieks just in case she woke the sleeping professor.

'Let me out! Let me out!' she hissed through the crack under the wardrobe door. 'I'll tell Mum.'

But Squidgy just laughed. He knew his great wick-

34

edness was actually inherited from his mother and she would be deeply proud of him for tricking his little sister and shutting her in a wardrobe.

'I'll let you out later,' he hissed back. 'Then – hey whacko – we can go home together, me holding the realer-than-real computer game, and you trailing after me, giving admiring glances at my back. Now, to work! To work!'

And he tiptoed back to the PIES AND BURGERS door.

'Some PIES AND BURGERS – I mean, SPIES AND BURGLARS – might be frightened away by a big KEEP OUT notice. But I am not the sort of villain who takes any notice of notices,' he muttered softly.

He had to search for his 'Open Sesame' door opener. In the excitement of his climb and of trapping his little sister in the wardrobe he had forgotten just which pocket he had hidden it in. But at last he found it jammed into the top of his boot (a favourite hiding place for villains wanting to conceal daggers and forged banknotes). Grinning with wickedness, he turned to the door.

That door was no match for an 'Open Sesame' door opener. It popped wide open, making the same sound as a cork leaping joyously from a bottle of rare champagne. Just for a moment Squidgy Moot hesitated, the smile frozen on his face, for he thought he had heard an echo bouncing back from the bedroom – an echo that sounded more like splintering timber than a champagne cork.

But even the sound of splintering timber does not delay a true villain for more than ten seconds. Looking around the room, Squidgy saw nothing to alarm him.

'It was probably just some dead branch falling off the internut,' he muttered to himself, and slipped into the darkness beyond the door.

At last, at last, he must be – he had to be – in Professor Mockery's laboratory.

'Hey whacko!' said Squidgy Moot, relaxing and slapping Formby on the shoulder. 'Well done! We can relax again.' He grinned triumphantly at Nina. 'Have fun in the wardrobe!'

'OK, you laugh while you've got the chance,' Nina cried. 'I'm going to tell Minnie, so watch out! Our revenge will be terrible!'

She stormed out of the room.

But Formby barely noticed her go. He was bent over his De Luxe Data Book, for now he had his trusty pen in his hand he just could not stop writing. The story had seized him in its teeth and he was captured by the excitement of it. The only way to find out what happened next was to keep writing, so Formby wrote on.

CHAPTER 11

Squidgy let the torchlight run around this new room. The walls seemed to be set with screens, all heavily framed and all turned off. Squidgy barely noticed them for he found himself confronted by a dozen strange shapes set out on special stands.

They must be inventions, he thought. Now which ones are worth stealing?

He knew the realer-than-real computer game would be a silver disk, easy to slide into the computer. And the helmet, which was part of the game too, would surely be easy to recognize. It would look like a space helmet of some kind, but it would have a plastic cord complete with power plug, leading out of one of its ears. Once he had put on the helmet and plugged it in, he would be transported into the realer-than-real world, and realer-than-real adventures would begin.

Yet none of the inventions in front of him looked in the least like silver disks or plug-in helmets. Indeed, as inventions go, they were puzzling. There was one that shone in the light of his torch like a double spiral of silver and gold. There was another that leaped up in a fountain of scarlet and emerald wire. How could glittering spirals and fountains possibly fit into a computer? How could they push a hard-working villain into that strange, electronic, realer-than-real computer game space? Yet Squidgy stared, transfixed, just as he had stared at the scribbles beside Professor Mockery's bed a few minutes earlier. That spinning spiral, that leaping fountain, made his own heart spin – made his own heart leap – and he couldn't work out why. For the second time in ten minutes he was filled with dreamy wonder, and when a villain is filled with dreamy wonder twice in ten minutes something peculiar is going on.

Luckily villains are quick to snap out of such moments.

'Stop it!' Squidgy ordered himself. 'Get on with what you came here to do! Find that realer-than-real disk, steal it, then shoot away out of here.' And within a second, Squidgy Moot became, once *more, the villain he had always planned to be.*

Formby put down his pen and looked at the new pages with satisfaction.

'A little sister locked in the wardrobe! A villain back on his villainous trail!' he cried. 'And, after I've had dinner and wiggled my fingers a little, I'll write the part where you find the disk. And if any more little sisters try to force their way into our story we'll push them all into wardrobes.'

'Yeah, about time too!' said Squidgy Moot. He was looking unexpectedly thoughtful. 'But what about these spirals and fountains and things? What's this dreamy wonder that keeps pushing its way in? I can't work it out.'

'Oh, forget the dreamy wonder!' said Formby rather impatiently, for he thought he deserved much more praise than he was getting. 'I somehow felt you mustn't find the helmet absolutely straight away, so I put the spirals and fountains in to take up a bit of space. Writers do that.'

'I can't just *forget* dreamy wonder,' objected Squidgy Moot. 'We villains don't want to be bothered with things like that, and yet, now you've written it in, I'm quite enjoying it.'

Formby stared at the notebook. He wasn't sure why he had put in moments of dreamy wonder into his story. Yet somehow it had felt right.

'I'm the boss of this story,' he cried at last. 'Don't bug me! If I want you to feel dreamy wonder then you've *got* to feel it. Anyhow I'm not changing it now. My hand's gone numb.'

'If I was an author,' sneered Squidgy Moot, 'I would never worry about a mere numb hand. I'd scribble on and on bravely, night and day, day and night, night and day, getting everything right first time.'

'Oh, shut up!' said Formby crossly.

Squidgy Moot stuck out his tongue, and disappeared.

Formby looked around his bedroom. Alone at last! But how could he hide his notebook so that Minnie would never find it?

As his eye ran along his bookcase, it fell on a book his aunt had given him two Christmases ago – *The Wonderful Adventures of Milly and Mark in Bunnyland.*

'Even Minnie wouldn't dream of reading about Bunnyland,' he muttered, and he whisked the cover away from *Milly and Mark* and clapped it on his De Luxe Data Book, which he then slid between two very good books about vampires . . . books he had read over and over again. Then, with a sigh of relief, he collapsed into a chair. The room felt peaceful and even sleepy, for big brothers were in charge of the story once more, while little sisters were safely shut up in wardrobes. That's the way stories should be, thought Formby.

After a while, he went downstairs and found Minnie colouring in a *Star Wars* poster with felt pens, while his mother and father watched an arts programme on television, pretending to be interested in culture in order to set a good example to their children.

Formby prepared to rush out of the room once more, but accidentally overheard something on the telly that made him hesitate. He stood for a moment, listening, then slowly sank into a nearby chair. His parents exchanged satisfied glances. Their plan was working. *Their dear son had suddenly become interested in art and refinement.* They smiled with pleasure, and prepared to put up with it themselves, all for the good of their darling son. As for Formby, he was so unexpectedly interested in what he was hearing that he did not notice Minnie leave her colouring in and sneak out of the room, taking a handful of felt pens with her.

CHAPTER 12

On screen, Mimi Rollick, the famous television front person, was interviewing the famous writer Mischa Slotkin, winner of the Nobel Prize for Bloodthirsty Stories.

'The story just flows out of me like good-quality tomato sauce from an "Eezi-squeeze" bottle,' Mischa Slotkin was saying. 'I merely write what the story tells me to write. If anything is ever wrong with one of my stories, it is all the story's own fault.'

'The story's fault?' cried Formby's father. 'How can it possibly be the *story's* fault?'

'You see, the characters in the story often try to boss me around,' said Slotkin, just as if he had heard

Mr Mackinaw. 'So when things go wrong I simply blame the characters.'

'Load of rubbish if you ask me!' said Formby's father, though no one *was* asking him. Formby's mother kicked him, reminding him to set a good example.

However, Formby's tired face had brightened. He wriggled his stiff fingers.

Hey! he thought. Mischa Slotkin blames the characters in the story if anything goes wrong. Great idea! I'll blame Squidgy Moot if things go wrong.

And the expression on his face could only be described as one of dreamy wonder.

Suddenly there was a curious flicker on the television screen. Just for a moment, it seemed to Formby that a wicked face winked at him over Mischa Slotkin's shoulder – winked, then gnashed its tusks, and *then* disappeared. It seemed to Formby that he was glimpsing – there, on ordinary family television – the wicked face of Count Aspio, the computer game villain. Formby's mouth fell open. Had he really seen, in real family life, the invention of an invention? He shook his head in bewilderment.

It was just as well that he did not know what was going on in his room at that exact moment. His little sister, Minnie, was searching desperately for the hidden De Luxe Data Book, and behind her, dancing up and down, kicking her zoot boots into the air, snapping her teeth and urging Minnie on, was none other than wicked Nina Moot.

CHAPTER 13

'How are you all getting on with your stories?' Miss Rogers asked the class, next day. 'Is anyone ready to *share* their stories yet, and then listen to helpful criticisms?'

Some goody-goodies began waving their stories at her, grinning and fawning. Formby smiled scornfully. He felt he had done enough sharing already, what with villains bullying him and little sisters getting in on the act. He made up his mind that, when the time came for him to share his story, he would not let anyone change a single word.

'And what about you, Formby Mackinaw?' asked Miss Rogers with a teacherly smile, sweet but as false as Great-grandpa Mackinaw's front teeth. She had noticed the scornful expression on Formby's face, and she did not care for it.

'My story's great, Miss Rogers,' said Formby. 'And if anyone finds anything wrong in my story it is the story's own fault, not mine. I heard that in an arts programme on television.'

'What?' cried Miss Rogers, leaping back in alarm. She hated it when kids turned out to be smarter than she was. All the same she couldn't argue with a television arts programme, so she did not force Formby to share his story, but let him get on with trying to draw pictures for it, which was good fun though the pictures did not work out as well as he had hoped.

School was over for the day. Formby fairly skipped across the playground and into the park. Once there, however, he took evasive action for fear of being bullied by Aspen Twinkler. Sliding secretly from tree trunk to tree trunk, he moved like a shadow past the cactus house. All in vain! Suddenly, Aspen Twinkler was looming over him, rubbing his hair the wrong way, elbowing him in the ribs and pulling a few school books out of his backpack.

'No use *you* going to the video arcade today,' Aspen said, 'because *I'll* be there, and I'm going to be at the video centre *all* afternoon. No room for *you*!'

'The video arcade!' cried Formby scornfully. 'Video games are nothing to the game *I'm* playing.'

Aspen Twinkler stared at him.

'What game?' he asked.

'None of your business,' Formby said. 'And, anyhow, you can keep those books. There's nothing in them but maths and stuff.'

Aspen Twinkler looked as if all the fun had suddenly gone from his life. His elbows twitched, almost as if he were trying to spike himself with them. Then he shrugged his shoulder three times, sneered, threw the books into the air and marched away. For some reason Formby felt he had won a victory, but he couldn't work out why or how.

'Traitor! Traitor! Alligator!' howled a new voice, and there, dancing like a savage dervish, was none other than Squidgy Moot himself, while at a distance, also dancing like a dervish – a smaller one but every bit as savage – was Nina Moot, somehow out of the cupboard and on the loose once more. 'You wrote *more* of the story after you pretended your hand had gone numb. Who said you could let Nina out of the wardrobe?'

'Ha ha ha-HA ha!' shouted Nina, making rude gestures, and dancing just out of reach of her wicked brother's long arm.

'Listen to her,' cried Squidgy. 'No villain wants to have a sister shouting "Ha ha ha-HA ha!" at him.'

But a terrible thought had occurred to Formby.

'Minnie!' he shouted. 'Minnie must have found my De Luxe Data Book inside the cover of *The Wonderful Adventures of Milly and Mark in Bunnyland.*' He entirely forgot about Aspen Twinkler and the video arcade. Instead he tore down the road, shot around the corner, raced along his own street, and in at his back door.

'Hello, darling,' said his mother, spilling her cup of tea in alarm at his noisy entrance. 'And how was school today?'

But Formby was rushing down the hall, making for his own room. He slammed the door after him, leaped for the bookshelf and ran his trembling finger across the backs of the books. Yes? No? Yes? No? No!

His De Luxe Data Book, folded in the *Bunnyland* cover, was nestling safely between the two well-loved vampire books.

Formby hastily turned to the last page, and gave a deep sigh of gratitude. The last words were *his* words, and in *his* handwriting too.

And yet . . . and yet Nina Moot, his villain's little sister, was certainly out in the world once more. How could she break out of the wardrobe without the writer's permission?

Formby's anxious eye roved around his room looking for clues. Suddenly he leapt to his feet with a cry of horror.

'My pen that writes in seven colours!' he cried. 'It's not here. Who's taken it?'

'Great!' said Squidgy Moot sarcastically, from somewhere behind him. 'I've got a writer who can't keep track of his own pen.'

Gritting his teeth, Formby carefully slid his De Luxe Data Book, folded in its *Bunnyland* cover, back into his collection of vampire books. Then he tiptoed down the hall and peeped into Minnie's room. It was empty. She was probably off with her friend Sandra. But had she written another chapter of the story, tricking it into doing what *she* wanted it to do by using *his* pen?

Lying on Minnie's pink desk, between the plastic spaceman with the zoot gun and her pale-blue plastic unicorn with flowers in its mane, was Formby's pen that wrote in seven colours. He snatched it up desperately. He had been writing in blood red when he last wrote anything, but now the pen was clicked to purple.

'So that's how Minnie has added a piece on to my story,' Formby hissed. 'Now where can she have hidden the piece she has added on?' He began to search wildly in her desk drawers, throwing out pages of notepaper with bunnies and Bambis in the top corner of each page (a present from a distant aunt who did not know Minnie at all well). He found a secret packet of jelly beans, and paused long enough to eat all the black ones by way of revenge. Then he swept on, crawling through Minnie's wardrobe, twisting among her dresses and overalls and kneeling on her shoes, and searching relentlessly. At last, he even wriggled under her bed, where he found a lot of dust and cat hair, but no hidden stories. By the time he pulled himself out, he was so covered with fluff and cat hair he looked rather like a fluffy alien from the planet Purr-Purr. He even had whiskers of thread and a moustache of duvet-down.

And then, just as he was about to groan and give up, Formby saw the corner of something sticking out from under Minnie's pillow. It was a girl's diary in a yellow plastic cover, and it was wound around with a green-velvet hair ribbon tied in an interknot like a nest of tiger worms.

With a yell of triumph Formby snatched it up and carried it back to his own room. After breaking a fingernail on the knot, he simply lost patience and tore the ribbon away. Then, collapsing in his chair, he began to read, and, as he read, he felt Squidgy Moot peering over his left shoulder and reading along with him so that, when they gasped in horror (which they were forced to do from time to time), they both gasped as one.

CHAPTER 14

Shut in the blackness of the wardrobe, the victim of a big brother's treachery, Nina Moot tried to work out just which way up she was. It was not easy. She had turned head over heels when Squidgy pushed her, and, not only that, she was made dizzy by the smell of socks and sneakers. Suddenly she remembered her shoes . . . a birthday present from her wicked godmother. After all, those shoes did fire zoot particles through the points in their toes.

Facing what she believed to be the wardrobe door, Nina wriggled her toes inside the shoes until they were poised over secret buttons set into the soles. Then she pressed down with her muscular big toes.

Fttttz! Fttttz! *Zoot particles shot out in two glittering streams.*

Faintly, she heard in the distance a door bursting open with the same sound a cork makes as it leaps joyously from the neck of a bottle of vintage champagne, but Nina's particular door stayed tightly closed. It was the wardrobe FLOOR that opened wide. It crackled; it splintered; it vanished away. Suddenly Nina was somersaulting down, down, down (a lot of shoes and socks falling around her). She was tumbling right through the hole in one floor, while, from far below, another floor was rising to meet her. Brave though she was, she couldn't help letting out an eagle-shriek of surprise. And her shriek was answered.

Crash! Thud-thud-thud-thud-thud!

The crash was not one of those hard, scraping crashes, however, but a soft, pillowy one! Nina had tumbled on to an unmade bed covered with blankets, duvets, and downy pillows. Thud-thud-thud! That was the sound of Professor Mockery's shoes raining down on top of her.

'Hey whacko!' *she exclaimed in despair, folding her arms over her head and shrinking down among the bedclothes.*

'Hey whacko to you too!' *said a voice.* 'Lovely of you to drop in!'

A woman, wearing a wide grin along with the white smock of a scientist, was peering at her over clever-looking glasses with thick, tortoiseshell rims.

'Most people – villains, spies, burglars and rascals of that kind – try to climb up the internut and blow up the door,' she said, helping Nina out from under the pillows and shoes, and standing her on her feet once more. 'You are the first one ever to come in through the ceiling.'

'Who are you?' asked Nina.

'I am Professor Mockery,' said the woman. Nina stared at her in amazement.

'But Professor Mockery is a man!' she cried. 'I have seen him on television collecting the Nobel Prize for the year's best computer game.'

A weary expression passed over the woman's face.

'That's another Professor Mockery – my big brother, Waldo,' she said. 'I am Elsivera. But people always think anyone with a moustache like Waldo's is bound to be a great inventor. People believe in mous-taches. Of course, I could easily invent a way to grow a moustache myself, but it would take up valuable inventing time and, by now, I can't be bothered.'

Nina looked around her. She was now in a huge, high room filled with mysterious scientific stuff. It must be behind one of the doors she had seen when climbing from the top to the bottom of the internut. At one end of this great room stood a machine shaped like a tubby spaceship and connected (by a lot of white, snaky extension cords) to a place in the wall where about six plugs clustered looking as if they were all trying to squeeze themselves into the one socket. Professor Elsivera saw Minnie notice this machine.

'By this time next year people all over the world will be connecting their computers to devices like that one,' she remarked, jerking her thumb at it carelessly. 'It's a wonderful new piece of computer-game technology. I call it the realer-than-real pod.'

Benches, covered with transistors, cryogenic units, microsonic relays and a few electron microscopes, ran around the room, while screens, set into the wall, were playing a variety of alarming video games, all with the sound turned off. Just inside the door stood a steel frame supporting a large helmet with blue goggles and with wires trailing from it. Beside this helmet stood a vast desk, which looked as big as a rugby field, and which was covered with crumpled newspaper.

Nina could see a loaf of French bread as long as a broomstick, a salt cellar, and a large 'Eezi-squeeze' bottle of tomato sauce. The wall behind the desk was covered with large, coloured pictures drawn with crayons and felt pens, and looking as if they had been left there for weeks. The biggest one showed a ferocious warrior with hairy ears, curling horns and remarkably sharp elbows. She recognized him at once – Count Aspio, the computer villain whose picture was painted on the outside of the Mockery house.

'Sorry about the mess,' said Professor Mockery, looking rather guiltily towards her desk. 'I don't really have time to cook, so I often make do with fish and chips, squirted all over with lashings of tomato sauce and an extra pinch of salt. And now, since you dropped in without letting me know you were coming, I am going to try out a segment of my new realer-than-real game on you.'

Before Nina could argue, Professor Elsivera had snatched up the helmet from the hatstand, popped it on Nina's head, slapped the tin ears over Nina's ears, flipped the goggles down over Nina's eyes, and had plugged Nina into the realer-than-real pod.

Nina turned cold with horror. Suddenly, directly in front of her (waving both a laser sword and a zoot gun), there appeared a warrior with hairy ears and curling horns. His bright-red eyes glittered with an evil, alien light. His elbows looked like swords. Behind him writhed a hundred spiked serpentine aliens with crests and fangs and glaring, yellow eyes shouting, 'Let me at her!' or, 'My turn to destroy a helpless victim!' And so on. As Nina stared in amazement, the warrior's red eyes blinked and he smiled an evil smile.

'I am the outer-space bully, Count Aspio,' he said in a lisping voice that seemed to have a little trouble sliding out around his tusks. 'Tell that professor out there that I am indeed becoming powerful. I'm going to break out of the computer-game world and, once I have shrugged my way out of the frail circuits she uses to trap me in this wretched game pod, I'll come roaring after her. I'll elbow her with my laser elbows. I'll toss her scientific notes into another dimension. Tell her to beware.'

He stretched out his hand, which had great, long, sharp nails on every finger, and he pointed his forefinger at Nina. Somehow Nina knew, at once, that those nails could be fired like arrows. Though normally very brave, she could not help letting out an eagle-shriek and swinging her arm across her face. To her surprise, a shield shaped like a dartboard was strapped to her arm. Bing! Bing! Bing! went the fingernail darts pinging into it.

But then she felt the helmet being whisked away. Her ears were free once more. The man with the hairy ears totally disappeared. The only person in the room with Nina was Professor Elsivera, once more holding the helmet.

'Did it seem to you as if you were actually having an adventure?' asked Professor Mockery, as Nina studied her own arm in amazement. No shield! No fingernail darts! All the same, something had happened. Nina's arm was covered in tiny scratches. She held it out to Professor Elsivera, who bent over it frowning.

'I saw a man with curling horns and sharp elbows,'

said Nina as Professor Elsivera studied the scratches. 'He told me his name was Count Aspio and said that he was becoming powerful. Then he stretched out his hand and fired fingernails at me. And just about that moment you took the helmet off and everything vanished,' Nina said, 'except for those little scratches.'

'Most curious,' frowned Professor Elsivera. 'I'd better check the circuits again. You see, Aspio is not real, no matter what he might try to tell you. He's just fooling himself if he thinks he is. Yet how could his darts possibly have scratched your arm so that the scratches show up here? It is most disturbing. Let me comfort you with gingernuts and orange juice.'

'I don't need comforting,' said Nina (but quickly accepted the orange juice and gingernuts just the same). 'I just want to know why there are two Professors Mockery, and why your brother wins prizes for inventing video games if it's really you who does all the inventing?'

'In the beginning', said Professor Elsivera Mockery, 'my brother, Waldo, and I were poor orphans. Our rich uncle, who looked after us, was a scientist and he desperately wanted my brother to be a scientist too. However, I was always miles better at science than Waldo.'

'I've noticed that little sisters are often cleverer than big brothers,' said Nina.

'My uncle wasn't interested in little sisters,' said Elsivera. 'I was lucky to have Waldo, who was pretty good as big brothers go. For instance, see that tatty old picture of Count Aspio pinned behind my desk? Waldo drew it especially for me years ago when I was five. I have treasured it ever since and used it as a model of wickedness in video games. I was the one who named it Count Aspio, but my brother was the one who invented the way Count Aspio looked.'

The picture flapped and seemed to snarl as she spoke Count Aspio's name.

'Anyhow, Waldo and I got into the habit of doing one another's work and, as we grew older, we kept on pretending to be one another. I enrolled for Art School while Waldo delighted my uncle by going to Science School. But, once school was over, we would tear home, secretly swap books and notes, and work until late at night on the things that we were really interested in. And that's how it came about that while Waldo was being presented with the Nobel Prize for Computer Games, I was accepting the Shiverfeather Art Prize.'

'It sounds confusing,' said Nina.

'Oh, it can be,' agreed Professor Elsivera. 'People come rushing up to Waldo talking about semiconductors, and he . . . well, poor Waldo still thinks semiconductors are very short men who work on trains. And, as for me, I have to listen to people exclaiming about the glory of my brush strokes. It's lucky we both enjoy trickery, jokes and secrets. Pretending to be one another keeps us entertained. But can it be that Count Aspio really has taken on a wicked computer life of his own?'

'I shall run at him with my zoot boots if I catch him trying to come after my big brother and me,' said Nina. 'Well, I will when they've had time to recharge themselves. I used a lot of zoot power in order to break out of the wardrobe and they've gone flat.'

'That's the style!' cried Professor Elsivera admiringly. 'Naturally I am opposed to needless violence, but there are times when big brothers certainly need little sisters to protect them. Have you finished your gingernuts and orange juice? Would you like some more?'

'No thank you,' said Nina, 'but I wouldn't mind playing another computer game – and all the way through this time. My brother is always making out he is the only person who can play computer games, and if I get some secret practice while I am here I might actually beat him.'

'A good idea!' said Professor Elsivera. 'We little sisters need to win from time to time, or big brothers start thinking they're the boss of the world. I will take notes on your reactions.'

She picked up a black, oblong shape that reminded Nina of a television-programme selector.

'There's a red switch on the wall over there,' she said to Nina. 'Just flip it down will you?'

Nina made for the red switch but as she reached for it, she saw something puzzling. There were two red switches. Which was the right one? Just to be on the safe side she switched them both down. As she did this, Professor Elsivera clicked her programme selector at a screen that was connected by various wires to the realer-than-real pod.

Twang! There was a curious sound... a musical explosion. It came so suddenly that both Professor Elsivera and Nina gave cries of alarm. Something had gone wrong. Their cries were greeted with a burst of ruthless laughter. A fountain of sparks burst out around the sides of the screen, while the great realer-than-real pod began an eerie dance on its short legs. As it rocked from side to side, an eerie red mist oozed out into the room, rather like tomato sauce from a faulty 'Eezie-squeeze' bottle. A hideous voice boomed at them. It was the voice of Count Aspio.

'At last! At last!' it cried. 'Someone has turned on both red switches. I have enough power... enough power! Here I come, bringing my laser sword and my electronic elbows with me.'

With these words, the whole pod split open like a ripe fig on a hot summer day. It was terrifying.

'Keep your distance,' cried Nina bravely, planning to fire a warning shot from her zoot boots. But the boots were not yet recharged properly. They made a particularly rude noise and went limp on Nina's feet. She had to curl her toes to keep them on.

'Oh dear,' said Professor Elsivera, as Count Aspio bore down on them. 'I think we're doomed.'

'Let's run!' cried Nina. 'You should always run when you're doomed. And my boots need another ten minutes to recharge. A bit of desperate running will help them.'

As she began to run (desperately) round and round the laboratory, she felt her faithful boots tighten up once more.

Count Aspio snarled, waved his laser sword and leaped towards them.

'Perhaps you're right,' said Professor Elsivera. She began to run too.

CHAPTER 15

'So Minnie has taken over the story again,' said
Squidgy Moot. 'And look what has happened. *Your*
little sister has somehow put *my* little sister in the
laboratory with the *actual* computer-game professor
who turns out to be a little sister herself. And they're
having adventures. Meanwhile I'm stuck upstairs
with a snoring brother who is a professor of the
wrong kind. Do something! Do something!'

'I can't tear these pages up or I'll damage the
story,' said Formby. 'I know! I'll *scribble* them out.'
He seized his pen.

'No!' yelled Squidgy Moot. 'No! Don't do that.
Scribbling-out would be agony to me and I can't

stand agony. Let's have revenge! Write the next chapter immediately. Change the story! And *then* make sure that your little sister can't get at either your pen or your De Luxe Data Book. I'll bet Shakespeare didn't leave his De Luxe Data Book *or* his pen lying around so his little sisters could get at them.'

Formby was amazed. Once the words were written down, they seemed to take on a strange life of their own. Sometimes it even seemed that the story was already alive and waiting in some other place – possibly the realer-than-real – sucking words *in* without once worrying about who was writing them *down*.

'Nina's *lucky*,' growled Squidgy Moot. '*She's* had the fun of zooting her way through the bottom of the wardrobe. Whereas *I've* had all the hard work of climbing the internut, not to mention moments of dreamy wonder, and I haven't had a single dangerous adventure so far.'

'Shut up!' Formby roared. He could feel himself glowing with fury. 'I need to think hard and you're putting me off with all your grizzling. Just *shut up!*'

There was a deep, dead silence. Formby tried to cram as much thinking into the silence as he possibly could. He knew it would not last long.

'That's it!' shouted Squidgy Moot suddenly. 'You've had thirty whole seconds. Shakespeare could have got ideas for ten plays in thirty seconds.'

'Shakespeare didn't know how to play video games the way I do,' shouted Formby, 'so I'm miles cleverer than Shakespeare. Anyhow I *have* got an idea, actually – a really good one too – good enough to count as *inspiration*. But it's an absolute, dead secret.'

'Tell me! You can trust me!' Squidgy Moot cried.

'No way!' exclaimed Formby. He *felt* smug. He *looked* smug. 'Just crawl back into the story right now. You'll feel the full force of my inspiration later this evening.'

And off he went, grinning craftily, certain he had a way to defeat Minnie at last.

That evening after dinner (while Minnie was in her room having a secret feast of jelly beans and wondering why there were no black ones), Formby slid up slyly beside his father.

'Dad!'

'Mmmm?' grunted his father, his eyes fixed on the television screen. Formby's parents were now watching a series about drug smugglers. Formby had often heard them telling other grown-ups that no one with any good sense would waste time watching this programme. However, when the right time came, they pulled the curtains across (so that no one looking in from the street could see them watching it), slumped down before the screen, and secretly enjoyed the excitement of it all.

'Dad, can I watch with you?'

'Certainly not!' cried Formby's father, sitting up much straighter in his chair. 'This is a programme of unsuitable violence. I wouldn't watch it myself, if your mother didn't enjoy it so much.'

'Oh, Dad, *do* let me watch,' moaned Formby, dancing in front of his father and making sure he was right in front of the screen.

'Don't pester me,' moaned his father, stretching his neck and swaying from right to left as he struggled to peer around Formby. 'Can't you find something useful to do?'

'Well, could I go into your office and work on your computer?' begged Formby. 'I know how to turn it on. I use computers at school.'

'Yes! Yes!' said Formby's father, anxious that his dear son should stop dancing in front of an unsuitable programme. Over Formby's shoulder he caught a glimpse of someone holding a plank with a nail in the end of it. 'Quickly! Off you go right now.'

So off went Formby. Out in the shadowy hall, Squidgy Moot appeared and began sliding along behind him.

'See how clever I was over that?' Formby muttered out of the corner of his mouth. 'Minnie is utterly forbidden to use the computer, because everyone knows little sisters are useless with technology.'

He quietly tiptoed into the office. The computer

sat by itself on a small table with a proper office whirl-around chair drawn up to it.

Formby turned it on. Lights flashed. Mysterious messages appeared, flickered, then vanished, as the computer warmed itself up. At last he was confronted by a wonderful blank screen. Formby suddenly felt full of pleasure. In behind that empty screen was a story longing to break through, and he, Formby, was just the one to help it.

But at that moment the screen gave a curious blue flash and began to fill with numbers – with zeros and ones – some of them crowding together while others separated out, so that within a second there were dark and light patches all over the screen. A face began to take shape . . . a face with hairy ears and curling horns. The eyes blinked. The mouth stretched into a wicked smile. The lips moved but there was no sound.

Then letters began to appear along the bottom of the screen, just as if Formby was tapping in a message.

Click on me! the letters said.

'No way!' cried Formby. The devilish black eyebrows rushed together and collided over the nose. At the bottom of the screen, new words formed.

You'll be sorry! I know you. You often invade my space with your video-game playing. I'll get my own back. Soon I will be invading your space and I will bring my elbows with me. You won't enjoy my *game. Aha! Aha!*

The face and the lines of print flashed and disappeared.

Formby sat back, puffing his cheeks out and staring at the empty screen.

'Did you see that?' he asked. 'Or did I dream it? Perhaps I did. It was Count Aspio. He isn't just an idea in the story. He is appearing in my real life, looking more and more like Aspen Twinkler.'

'Forget your real life!' commanded Squidgy Moot. 'Don't be selfish! Get on with the story, but – hey – no falling on to beds for me. I hate bouncing about. Make something exciting happen to me in the art gallery . . . something much too exciting for a little sister to bear . . . but definitely no beds!'

'I'll begin with a "meanwhile",' Formby promised him.

CHAPTER 16

Meanwhile, Squidgy Moot, still exploring the top of the Mockery house, had suddenly leaped backwards with a cry of fear. It had seemed, for a moment, that wicked Count Aspio himself was looking in at him from one of the screens on the wall. There was that ugly face with its pointed teeth and straggling hair; there were its laser elbows. And then, for the first time since he had come into that room, Squidgy Moot understood that the dark, heavily framed screens around the walls were not screens at all. They were large pictures. He was in an art gallery of some kind.

Though this Count Aspio was a mere painting, he

was so well painted Squidgy could scarcely bear to look at him. Swivelling his green eyes, he looked uneasily at the picture next to it. Once again he leaped backwards with a cry of fear. Just for a moment he was convinced he was accidentally looking into a mirror. Then he saw that it was not a mirror but yet another picture – a totally unexpected one.

'It's a picture of ME,' Squidgy muttered to himself. 'It's a copy of that poster that was pasted on the post-office wall. What's it doing here?'

And now he noticed, also for the first time, a small table in one corner of the room, overflowing with squeezed tubes of paint, brushes, and bottles of turpentine. He looked back at the unexpected picture, concentrating hard. 'I look a lot worse than that,' he thought indignantly. 'My teeth are much more pointed, and my eyes are like laser beams. Here! Where are those brushes?'

He was so angry at seeing a picture of himself that did not show his true wickedness, that he totally forgot the picture of Count Aspio and, indeed, everything else in that strange room.

Grabbing paints and a paintbrush from the smeary table, Squidgy Moot leaped up on to the chair and quickly began to improve the picture.

'I'll show them,' he muttered. 'I'll show them.'

His brush, loaded with bright paint, flickered over the portrait. He leaped and darted like a swordsman

68

fighting a duel, concentrating hard – so hard he did not notice a sudden silence. The thunderous snoring had stopped. But all Squidgy could think of was the picture in front of him. At last, narrowing his eyes, he leaped back off the chair and studied his work. His smile widened. There was no doubt about it – due to his own skilful painting the picture looked much more villainous than it had only a few moments earlier. Hey whacko! he thought. I'm really good at this.

There was a rapid rushing sound behind him. Something like a great flopping wing came down over him. Arms like bands of steel closed around him. Something or someone swept Squidgy Moot off his feet, and hoisted him into the air.

'Help!' screamed Squidgy Moot, for he was sure Count Aspio had suddenly broken out of the portrait and seized him. And he struggled in a grip so ruthless he felt his nose going numb.

CHAPTER 17

Formby pushed the whirl-around chair back, then whirled around on it twenty-seven times.

'Bingo!' he cried.

'Now hang on a bit!' cried Squidgy Moot, trying to slow him down. 'This is getting out of hand. All I want to do is to steal that realer-than-real computer game, sell it for hundreds of thousands of dollars and make off into the Wild Unknown. Of course I'm glad I improved that picture though,' he added in an unexpectedly thoughtful voice.

'Shall I make you *steal* it?' offered Formby. 'You could probably sell it to a secret collector for a million dollars.'

Squidgy Moot staggered as if the Sludge Dragon of Pong the sewerage planet had suddenly breathed on him.

'What?' he cried. 'Do you mean someone would pay a million dollars for a mere picture?'

'Galleries and museums do it all the time,' said Formby. 'Pictures aren't just pictures. They're art.'

'I didn't know you could get *money* through art,' Squidgy Moot cried. 'I thought you had to be a villain to become rich. Rescue me from Count Aspio! Don't leave me dangling! Get my feet back on to the floor.'

'Formby,' called his mother's voice, for the unsuitable television programme was over and she was on her motherly warpath again. 'Formby, it's bedtime.'

'Hey whacko!' cried Squidgy Moot in despair.

But Formby carefully saved his chapter, giving it the file name MOOT. Then he pressed the proper buttons and his father's laser printer winked a little red eye at him. Within a few minutes Formby was holding his new chapter printed out on pure-white pages. It looked so good. But he was totally exhausted, worn out by literature and all the argument that went along with it, so he went to bed where he slept all night. Though Squidgy Moot did his best to get into his dreams and complain about the story, Formby was so tired that all his efforts were in vain and Squidgy was left dangling, hating every minute of it.

CHAPTER 18

The following morning, as Formby went to school, a hand descended on his backpack, and then an elbow jabbed him in the ribs. Of course it was Aspen Twinkler, suddenly being a morning bully as well as an after-school one.

'Have you chickened out on video games?' he cried. 'Don't blame you! You'll never be as good as me.'

'I'm doing something that's miles more fun than video games,' said Formby bravely, though he knew it might lead to more elbowing. '*You* couldn't do what I'm doing – not in a million years.'

'Homework?' cried Aspen, and with the skill of

a bully who has had a lot of practice, he twitched the new chapter from Formby's backpack, for Formby, who was only bothered about *after*-school bullying, had foolishly forgotten to zip his backpack shut that morning. 'Are you doing homework like a little goody-goody?'

Then Aspen read the first line aloud trying to make fun of it, but Formby noticed he tripped over the words every now and then.

'A little before this fearsome event, Squidgy Moot was up on the fifth floor,' read Aspen, and his mouth fell open. He came to a standstill. 'What fearsome event?' he cried as if he could hardly believe what he was reading.

'None of your business,' Formby shouted, trying to snatch his story back. But Aspen simply stepped away, holding the pages high above Formby's head and reading them as quickly as he could.

'Who *is* this wicked Count Aspio?' he asked.

Formby looked at the pages in Aspen's hand, then thought of the computer in his father's office at home. Really he had nothing to worry about. The entire chapter was safely stored inside the computer and he could easily run off another copy. He stepped out of Aspen's reach, laughing as he did so.

'Keep it and read it,' he shouted. 'You might learn something, and that would be pretty remarkable for someone who thinks with their elbows.'

Then, feeling he'd been brave enough, considering

how early in the day it was, he raced away at top speed leaving Aspen behind him.

He had only just settled down at his desk when Miss Rogers came dancing into class, very active and alert because of all the coffee she had been drinking in the staffroom.

'Now, how are those books coming along?' she asked.

'I have written fourteen pages,' said Lorna Winkle, a well-known goody-goody.

'My story is five pages long, but I am drawing great pictures,' said Johnny Knocks. 'And I've drawn three dinosaurs . . . a triceratops, a T-rex and a –'

'Formby,' said Miss Rogers with a knowing smile, 'how are *you* coming along with *your* story?'

Everyone looked at Formby. He could easily see that no one believed he had written a single page.

'I don't know how long my story is,' he said. 'Chapters one and two are in my De Luxe Data Book. Chapter three is in a diary with a yellow cover, and chapter four is on my father's computer.'

Miss Rogers was amazed to think that a computer-game boy like Formby could possibly have written four chapters.

'I'll believe in your four chapters when I see them,' she said in a suspicious voice. 'And I don't want to read chapters one and two of the story in one book, then have to look in another book for chapter three, and *then* have to look on a computer for chapter four. It would be impossible to shelve a story like that in the library. I want all your chapters in the same book, Formby.'

'But the story keeps darting in all directions,' said Formby.

'Be firm!' said Miss Rogers. 'Show the story who's boss. Do remember, Formby, we need books for the library.'

'I'll do my best,' said Formby with a sigh. 'Try writing a story yourself and see how you get on,' he mumbled, when he knew she couldn't hear him.

CHAPTER 19

After school, Formby set off for home planning to dart from bush to bush, hiding from Aspen as he crossed the park, but, before he so much as reached the park gates, he heard his name called and saw Aspen pelting after him. This was unusual. Up until now Aspen had always hidden and jumped out on him.

'Ooo-er!' Formby mumbled, and tried to run faster, but Aspen cut him off about seven steps before the park gates.

What was this? Aspen was not looking fierce or tormenting. Indeed he seemed rather anxious and was keeping his elbows tucked well in at his sides.

'Hey, kid!' he said (trying to sound like the *Star Wars* hero, Han Solo, talking to the main *Star Wars* hero, Luke Skywalker). 'No hurry, eh? Just tell me what was going on in that story you lent me this morning?'

'Lent you?' cried Formby. 'You *stole* it.'

'Yeah! Yeah!' said Aspen. 'I know I did sort of *borrow* it. But what happens next? And how does it begin?'

By now they were strolling through the park side by side, almost as if they were friends.

'Our class has to write a story for the school library,' Formby said. 'That's a bit of the story I was writing. And I have to get home and get on with it or my little sister will find it and muck it up again. Little sisters are the biggest pains in the world.'

'They're nothing to *big* sisters,' said Aspen with such deep feeling that Formby was startled.

'Little sisters *must* be worse than big ones,' he declared.

'I've got both sorts,' said Aspen. 'Big ones *and* little ones. And big ones are a hundred times worse. They are all terminators. Now, listen! If you bring me the rest of the story tomorrow morning I'll read it during Social Studies, and tell you what I think of it later.'

Formby hesitated. Aspen looked anxious.

'I'll let you have a turn at a video game tomorrow

77

afternoon, if you let me read the rest of your story,' he said. 'I want to know how what's-his-name – Squidgy Moot – gets away from thingummy . . . you know . . . What's-his-name . . . Count Aspio! Yeah man! Count Aspio! He sounds cool.'

'OK,' said Formby. 'I'll just go home and do the next bit and then I'll have it to show you tomorrow.'

When they parted on the other side of the park, Aspen gave Formby a thumbs-up sign.

'Just hang on in there!' he cried. 'That's what writing dudes like Shakespeare would do.'

Wonders never cease, Formby thought. Even Aspen knows about Shakespeare. Then he raced home, rescued his De Luxe Data Book in its false cover, re-stole Minnie's yellow diary and sneaked into the office. He booted up the computer. *Retrieve Document?* it asked him politely.

Formby's fingers twinkled briefly over the keyboard – MOOT! He pressed the ENTER button.

Yesterday's chapter leaped into life on the screen. It was like magic.

Formby had not really *studied* it properly yesterday. He had been too anxious to get it into the computer, saved and safe from little sisters. It was true he had taken his pen back, but a little sister like Minnie might easily find another way to worm herself into the story if he did not protect it. Formby stared at the blue screen.

This story looked just so *good* in that neat white

print. Any library would be delighted to have such a story on its shelves. Instead of going on with the next chapter he began to copy the whole story so far on to the computer, even though it annoyed him to include the chapters Minnie had written. It took him ages to work his way through first the De Luxe Data Book and then the diary.

As he finished at last, he felt someone sliding around the room behind him. He did not have to turn to know who was reading over his shoulder.

'Why aren't you getting on with the story?' asked Squidgy. 'I've been dangling around, hoisted into the air by Count Aspio since last night. Don't you care?'

'Sorry,' said Formby. 'I just thought I'd put the whole story on the computer before I went on with the next chapter. Doesn't it look great?'

Squidgy narrowed his green eyes.

'It *does* look good,' he agreed, rather unwillingly. 'Almost as good, in its way, as my picture did. You know, while I've been dangling, I've had time to *think*. Well, thinking is almost all you *can* do when you have to spend a whole night hoisted mid-air, though there is someone running round and round in circles somewhere on the floor below and sometimes that has distracted me. Anyhow, I've been thinking about that picture I improved when-ever the sound of those desperately running feet faded for a moment or two. Thanks to you, painting has been more fun than anything else in the story . . . more fun than wickedness.'

'You certainly made the picture look a lot more like you,' said Formby, anxious to keep him happy.

Squidgy began strutting around the room, smiling to himself and glancing at his reflection every time he passed the tennis cup that Mr Mackinaw had won in his distant youth, and which was kept highly polished. Meanwhile, Formby turned back to the computer, eager to begin a new chapter of the story.

CHAPTER 20

'Quickly, before I tear you apart,' roared a sinister voice. 'Are you a burglar or an art critic?' Squidgy Moot could not believe his ears. The voice was sinister all right but it was not the voice of Count Aspio. Squidgy suddenly understood. He was being hoisted into the air by Professor Mockery. Who would have thought that a man with a moustache like that could have muscles as well?

'I'm an art lover! An art lover!' cried Squidgy Moot, anxious to reassure the powerful professor whose moustache was tickling his ear.

Professor Mockery let him thump on to the floor in a tangled heap.

'What? A genuine art lover climbing the internut and sneaking into my studio late at night?' he exclaimed in an altered voice. 'I suppose it's possible. Stand up and let me look at you more closely.'

'I was hungry for art,' mumbled Squidgy Moot, thinking quickly. 'I just longed to see your wonderful paintings.'

'And what did you think of them?' cried Professor Mockery.

'They filled me with dreamy wonder,' said Squidgy Moot quickly.

There was a dead silence. Squidgy dared to shoot a sly glance at Professor Mockery. A broad, beaming smile was creeping out from under the moustache, just as sunshine might creep from under ragged, grey storm clouds.

'An art lover!' the professor exclaimed. 'A true art lover! Yes! Now I look at you more closely, I can see you really are an art lover. I thought, at first, you were a mere burglar trying to steal one of my sister's scientific secrets. We do get them dropping in from time to time. Stand up. Don't be shy!'

Squidgy staggered to his feet.

'I did wonder if I had wandered – accidentally wandered – into a scientific laboratory,' he said with great cunning.

'Oh, I do take my inspiration from science,' said Professor Mockery, 'and science often takes its inspiration from art. It's a great circle. My little sister, for example, has used my ideas in the various video and computer games she has invented, and I use her scientific ideas in my pictures.'

'Did you say something about having a little sister?' asked Squidgy in dismay.

'Yes,' said Professor Mockery. 'Elsivera! And she can be a great pain sometimes. But I don't suppose you have any idea what little sisters can be like.'

'I certainly do,' cried Squidgy with such sincerity that the professor beamed even more broadly.

'I see we have a lot in common,' said Professor Mockery. 'Which of my pictures is your favourite?' he asked, sounding greedy for praise, as artists sometimes are.

'I think this one is sensational,' Squidgy Moot said, pointing at his own portrait. 'Where did you get the idea for such a wonderful picture?'

'Ah! That one!' cried Professor Mockery. 'You have chosen well. It is an impression of the famous villain Squidgy Moot. I have never met him, of course, but I have been haunted by the poster the police pasted on to the post-office wall. That picture stands for doom and danger ... for the dark side of life. I haven't got it quite right yet, but it's getting there ...' He broke off, looking at the picture, and his expression changed. 'Though it looks a lot better than I remembered. How amazing! Perhaps I improved it in my sleep. We artists often do things in our sleep that wide-awake people wouldn't think of doing. Perhaps I should sleep more often. In fact,' he went on, sounding excited, 'the longer I look at this picture the more clearly I see that it is out and away the best thing I have ever done. I have a feeling that I will bask in glory because of this painting. I'll probably make a lot of money out of it.'

A spasm flickered across Squidgy's countenance. He opened and shut his mouth a few times as if he had suddenly seen his own face, smiling back at him from a golden frame glittering with diamonds.

'You know, there is a distinct resemblance,' said Professor Mockery, peering from Squidgy Moot to the picture and then back to Squidgy once more. 'Is it possible that ... I mean, can it be that you — you — are actually Squidgy Moot himself?'

'It can! I am!' said Squidgy, strutting a little. 'I am an art lover and a villain as well.'

'Oh, what glory!' shouted the professor. 'My pictures must have become valuable enough for a Squidgy-Moot class of villain to steal.'

But at that moment every picture on the gallery walls began to rattle like false teeth chattering at the South Pole.

'That's my sister!' cried Professor Mockery, spinning around. 'What does she think she's doing now? Oh, it's terrible the way a scientist makes pictures rattle on walls, and then hang crookedly. I'm always trying to straighten my art.'

'That's my sister!' yelled Squidgy Moot, leaping

In the air. 'I shut her in the wardrobe, and she's probably trying to get out. I mean, it sounds as if someone somewhere is running in circles, and it's rattling the whole house.'

He ran from the gallery to the bedroom next door.

'Stop it!' he yelled, flinging the wardrobe door open.

But what was this? The wardrobe was empty. There was no one and nothing in it – not unless you counted the big hole in the wardrobe floor.

'That wasn't there before,' cried Squidgy Moot.

Then, through that hole, far, far below, he caught a glimpse of his little sister, together with a strange woman. They seemed to be running in circles, looking anxiously over their shoulders as they ran. He saw them both quite plainly through the hole in the wardrobe floor and then they vanished, though the sound of running still beat at his ears.

'What's Elsivera running away from?' asked Professor Mockery, peering over Squidgy's shoulder. 'Really, you would think that even a little sister like her would have more sense by now.'

Then, far below, a sinister shape suddenly sprang into the centre of that hole, framed by broken boards – all that was left of what had once been a perfectly serviceable wardrobe floor.

Both big brothers gasped in horror.

'Count Aspio!' they cried as one big brother.

'Nina!' shouted Squidgy Moot. 'Why doesn't she fire her zoot boots?'

'Elsivera!' gasped the professor. 'Confound it, I'll have to rescue her. That's the trouble with little sisters. You have to rescue them in moments of crisis. Will you jump down first, or shall I?' he added with old-world courtesy.

'Er . . .' mumbled Squidgy. Of course he was keen to rescue Nina, but it was a long way down.

As he hesitated, Nina ran into sight once more. She turned. She leaped. She kicked her feet into the air.

There was a flash of eerie light. Two streams of glittering particles arched through the air. Squidgy Moot knew immediately what had happened.

Nina had fired her zoot boots. And, to his horror, Squidgy Moot felt the floor next to the wardrobe – the very floor on which he was kneeling – groaning, tilting, then shivering to bits beneath him and beneath Professor Mockery too. For Nina had missed Count Aspio and hit the ceiling above her, and in certain houses a sister's ceiling can be a brother's floor. Squidgy Moot and his new friend and admirer, Professor Mockery, finding they had nothing left to kneel on, had no choice but to tumble into open space, both screaming as they fell.

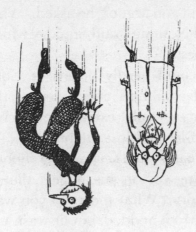

CHAPTER 21

Having got the story to this stage, Formby carefully printed it out twice – once for himself and once for Aspen Twinkler. He showed it to Squidgy Moot, thinking his villain would be delighted.

But Squidgy Moot seemed strangely absent-minded. Formby nudged him.

'See?' he said. 'I told you I'd fix things. I can't cut little sisters out of the story altogether, but I've given *you* the glory of rescuing them from danger. And I've added in a crumbling floor and a fall into darkness so the chapter will have a dangerous and exciting ending.'

'Fair enough!' said Squidgy. But he sounded as if he did not care.

Formby was taken aback.

'Why don't you argue?' he asked. 'What's wrong?'

'Nothing! Nothing!' said Squidgy Moot. 'Do what you think best.'

Formby could hardly believe it. Squidgy Moot had argued with him every step of the way, yet suddenly, at a really exciting moment, it almost seemed as if he had lost interest.

'Zoot streams and crumbling floors,' Formby said, counting off on his fingers the good things about his story. 'What more do you want?'

Squidgy Moot nodded, but he wasn't really listening. Feeling rather disappointed, Formby began searching his father's desk for a paper clip big enough to hold all his pages together. Squidgy suddenly spoke.

'Hey you!' he said to Formby.

Aha! We're going to have a fight after all, thought Formby with relief.

'What's wrong now?' he asked, quickly putting on the expression of a writer preparing for an argument.

'Do artists have teeth like mine?' asked Squidgy.

'Artists?' cried Formby, taken aback.

'I really enjoyed painting that picture,' said Squidgy. 'I wouldn't mind painting another one. Work more painting into the story.'

'Come off it! You're the villain . . . the *villain*!' snapped Formby. 'And I am only interested in computer games.' And then he paused, frowning. Was this still true? He certainly felt interested in his story. As he puzzled about this, he saw Squidgy Moot grow misty around the edges, and begin floating towards the computer. 'Where are you going?' he cried.

'I just thought I'd slide into the computer and float down the telephone wires,' said Squidgy Moot. 'I am going to travel by Internet, and when I arrive at the library computer I'm going to get off and check up on art. A million dollars for a painting! Hey whacko!'

'Not *every* painter gets paid a million dollars,' said Formby. 'Only famous *dead* ones!' But Squidgy had already disappeared and without so much as saying thank you to the writer who had given him (and all without meaning to), a totally new interest in life.

CHAPTER 22

Next morning on the way to school, Formby gave his first set of printed-out pages to Aspen, who snatched it eagerly saying, 'Thanks, kid!' almost as if they were friends, entirely forgetting about any elbowing or backward hair-ruffling. The second set he passed over to Miss Rogers at mid-morning break. She nearly fell over backwards.

'Do you mean I have to read all this fine print?' she gasped. Of course the goody-goodies had written stories, but their stories were filled with lots of coloured pictures, drawn big to take up room. Some of them had stretched out their writing too. Formby looked over at these stories scornfully. He could easily tell that the goody-goodies weren't serious about literature or art.

Miss Rogers had certainly not expected anyone in the class to write so much. As he watched her amazement, Formby was surprised to find that now he had written so much of his story, he suddenly wanted someone – anyone – to read it eagerly and tell him how good it was. But he also knew he had to approach Miss Rogers carefully.

'Just read the first three lines,' he suggested carelessly. Miss Rogers gave him a suspicious look, and began.

It was the blackest night that ever was. Lightning stabbed down into the city. Thunder rattled the roofs.

Of course, once she had begun reading she could not stop. She walked to her morning coffee with her nose a mere inch from the printed words, banging into other teachers as she went, and trampling on the occasional pupil. When mid-morning break was over, Miss Rogers was late back to class, and, as she looked at Formby, her spectacles went all smeary with emotion.

'You know, Formby,' she said, 'we teachers struggle on, and sometimes we wonder if it is all worthwhile. But a story like yours restores our faith in our work – and in literature too. Mostly I can guess the end of a story, but I must admit I have no idea of just how yours is going to end. Tell me at once! What happens?'

'Aha!' said Formby mysteriously. He did not want to tell Miss Rogers that he had no idea how it was going to end either.

'What about this Count Aspio? Will he actually become realer-than-real?' Miss Rogers asked. 'I already know ideas, games and real life all run into each other. But I feel I already know Count Aspio. For some reason he reminds me of that boy in Miss Armitage's class . . . what is his name? Oh, I remember. Aspen Twinkler! But I *must* know what happens next. Come on, Formby! Give me a clue.'

'Aha!' said Formby again, but his second 'Aha!' sounded much less certain than his first 'Aha!'

Miss Rogers grew suddenly aware of indignant silence in the classroom. She looked up to find that all the goody-goodies were staring at her disapprovingly. Everyone could see she was spending valuable classroom time talking to Formby Mackinaw, instead of concentrating on well-behaved pupils who really deserved her attention.

'Now, children,' she said quickly, 'look at the story Formby has written for the school library.' She held up his pages. 'I want all of you to do just as well as Formby. Formby, you have special permission to work on your story for the rest of the morning. And then bring it to me, for I must find out what happens next.'

Formby took his pages back to his desk. He began to read his own story, admiring the way its words fitted into one another, and quite forgetting that his little sister had written half of it for him. He found he could not really write any more while he was sitting at his school desk surrounded by jealous goody-goodies, so once again he tried to do some illustrations. But they just *would* not work out the way he wanted them to, though he tried them this way then that way until the bell rang for lunchtime.

He was longing to boast to Squidgy Moot about how he had impressed Miss Rogers with his story. But, strangely enough, though he looked keenly right and left as he dodged through the park later that afternoon, there was no sign of Squidgy Moot at all. He did see Aspen Twinkler walking slowly through the park, reading slowly, and stopping every now and then to point to some line. He did not seem in the least interested in bullying anybody. Nor did he look as if he was planning to go to the video arcade either.

As Formby watched cautiously, he saw Aspen look up from the pages. Their eyes met. Aspen's face brightened. A beaming smile spread from ear to ear.

'Hey, kid!' he called. 'Let me show you what I've been doing during maths. Drawings for your story. I even drew some at lunchtime too. I thought it needed drawings, so I did some.'

'Hold one up,' said Formby, anxious not to put himself in Aspen's elbow-range. Aspen shuffled among the papers, then held up a drawing in black and purple felt pen.

Formby gasped.

That drawing was amazing. It showed Squidgy Moot scrambling up the internut, and every little bit of it was exactly right.

'Hey!' he cried to Aspen. 'You're an artist as well as a bully. If you do more pictures for my story, it's certain to be put in the school library.'

'We're a team,' cried Aspen. 'Give me five!'

And their hands clapped together overhead in a moment of rare fellowship.

CHAPTER 23

Formby arrived home to find his mother gossiping with a neighbour. They had both been watching the famous afternoon soap opera called *Velveteen* on television. It was about two families who ran rival dance studios, and the mother of one family was giving secret tango lessons to the brother of the wife of the man who was father to most of the second family.

'But Hurley was never really *married* to Merlie,' Formby's mother was saying. 'They only pretended to be married so he could charge her against income tax.'

'No, don't you remember?' cried the neighbour.

'They *pretended* to pretend so that Lurlie wouldn't get jealous and refuse to close the deal with Berli. They wanted to make sure the tap-dancing course with Firlee went ahead as planned.'

'Where's Minnie?' Formby asked.

'Oh, she came home and ran straight off to the library,' his mother said, her head still full of *Velveteen*.

Formby raced into his father's office and switched on the computer. There was that strange blue flash and immediately the picture of Count Aspio began to fill the screen, but Formby was too quick for it, and he hastily hit RETRIEVE FILE with a bold finger. Count Aspio snarled at him, but Formby tapped in the file name MOOT, and Count Aspio was forced back behind the lines of neat printing.

There was Formby's story. How great it looked! But there was no time to read it now.

Quickly, he shot to the end of the story, anxious to get on with the next chapter. Then he gasped in amazement, for the end was not the end he had written only the night before. The names of Elsivera Mockery and Nina Moot danced before his eyes. How had they managed to muscle in here on his father's computer, particularly as Minnie was forbidden to touch it?

'Dreadful, isn't it?' said a voice beside him. He turned, and there stood Squidgy Moot looking every bit as furious as you would expect. And yet . . .

and yet . . . wasn't there still something just a little absent-minded about him? Didn't he look as if (though of course he was angry at little sisters pushing their way into the story) he was really thinking of something else? And he looked different in other ways too. For one thing he had a black eye. Well, that was only to be expected. Villains frequently have black eyes and broken noses, due to some act of wickedness that has gone wrong halfway through. But Squidgy Moot was now sporting a black beret on his wild hair, and his shirt and blue pants had been replaced with a floppy smock and velvet trousers. He wore a paintbrush, dripping with red paint, stuck behind his ear.

But there was no time to argue over the velvet trousers and the paintbrush.

'Minnie!' Formby exclaimed, pointing at the new print on the screen. 'I shall tell my father that she has been sneaking in here and using the computer without permission.'

'But she hasn't,' said Squidgy Moot. 'She's using the computer in the children's room at the public library to break into this computer here,' Squidgy said. 'Minnie has become a *hacker.*'

'I didn't know Minnie could hack,' cried Formby. 'How did you find out what she was up to?'

Squidgy Moot laughed bitterly.

'Remember I told you I was going to go to the library to do a bit of research on art?' he said.

'Well, I was just shooting along through the Internet cables, minding my own business, and I met Minnie's piece of the story coming the other way. I ran straight into it – a head-on collision! I tell you, Formby, it's a jungle in there.'

'Did the story give you that black eye?' asked Formby.

'Yes, but forget my black eye!' Squidgy exclaimed. 'We villains expect a few black eyes from time to time. Just read what your little sister has written and then get us out of this new tangle. You're the author! It's your job to rescue your villain when the story, not to mention the house, starts falling to bits around him.'

So Formby started to read Minnie's new Internet chapter.

CHAPTER 24

As the ceiling crumbled in Elsivera's laboratory, the hideous red mist drifted out of the broken pod. And then, suddenly, the terrible figure of Count Aspio came leaping through the mist, straight for Nina and Professor Elsivera. How fearsome he looked as he flew through the air, waving his laser sword in one hand and his zoot gun in the other. His bronzed arms were knotted, on either side of his elbows, with muscles as big as ripe watermelons.

'At last!' he shouted. 'At last! I have made the right connection. Ever since I was first drawn, I have been part of a stupid game for little children, but now I can take over everything – this story

first, then all the stories on television, then the story of the world, and then the story of the whole universe. I will be the master of all stories.' He fired his zoot gun into the air filling the great, echoing laboratory with laser-light.

'Turn him off! Turn him off!' yelled Nina.

Professor Elsivera ran to pull the six plugs clustered around the socket in the wall.

'Too late! Much too late,' yelled Aspio with a mocking laugh. He fired his zoot gun first at the plugs, and then at the two red switches beside Nina.

'Take that!' he cried. A flaring stream of zoot particles struck the plugs before Professor Elsivera reached them. She fell on her knees beside the power point, then looked over at Nina with a face the colour of wallpaper paste.

'All the plugs have melted into the master plug, and the master plug has melted into the socket. I can't unplug him now. Oh, I should have been much more careful.' The extension cords all began lashing like rats' tails.

'Don't panic!' Nina Moot yelled to Professor Elsivera, leaping high, and clicking the heels of her zoot boots together mid-leap. 'Little sisters will save the world.'

She kicked up her feet and a stream of zoot particles shot from her toes. But Count Aspio deflected them with his laser sword, and they streamed upwards at a sharp angle, striking the ceiling above close to the hole she had made escaping from the wardrobe in the first place. The ceiling crumbled more dangerously than ever. And at that moment, from somewhere above them all, came a shriek of despair. No! Two shrieks! Screams really!

CHAPTER 25

'This is terrible!' cried Formby. 'Minnie is only a little sister and she has lost control of the story. You must rescue her and rescue the story too.'

Squidgy Moot took action. He pushed Formby out of the whirl-around chair and leaped into his place in front of the computer.

His fingers twinkled over the keys.

CHAPTER 26

Squidgy Moot and Professor Waldo Mockery plummeted down like angels who have used so much energy doing good deeds that their wings have lost all flap-power. Down ... down ... they plunged into the laboratory below, screaming every inch of the way!

CHAPTER 27

'Hey whacko!' Squidgy cried triumphantly, spinning himself round and round on the whirl-around chair. 'Action! Poetry! Your turn now!'

Formby took a deep breath and tried to *think carefully* – something that authors, distracted by the excitement of their own stories, find very hard to do.

'And no shooting or zooting into the air now the ceiling is full of holes,' Squidgy Moot shouted. 'I don't want that good picture of me – the one I improved so much – to suffer zoot-damage.'

Formby turned on him. He saw with amazement that, though his hair was still like black fur,

104

Squidgy's teeth were not quite as much like fish teeth as they had been. Even his wicked expression seemed to have changed.

'What's *wrong* with you?' he cried. 'You said you wanted wickedness and glory, and now you're turning into a sort of hero.'

'I am *not*!' Squidgy cried, deeply insulted. 'But now I want to show my wickedness and glory in the pictures I paint, and then to sell them for a million dollars each.'

'But villains can't be *artists*,' Formby said disapprovingly.

'Who says?' yelled Squidgy. 'Lots of people have two jobs. Stop talking like a . . . a goody-goody.'

'I am not a goody-goody,' roared Formby, turning red with fury.

'Goody-goody!' sneered Squidgy, dancing a mocking dance just out of Formby's reach. Then his expression changed and his eyes popped.

'Hey!' he cried in a suddenly altered voice. 'Look! The story is going on under its own steam.'

Formby swivelled round and stared incredulously at the computer screen.

Words, line after line of them, were appearing on the screen . . . words which Formby certainly had not planned. Yet there they were, marching along like well-behaved cows at milking time.

'Minnie!' Formby hissed. 'She must be using the library computer to hack into the story.'

'Shut up and read,' said Squidgy Moot, 'and we'll strike back as soon as there is something to strike at.'

CHAPTER 28

'Your end has come, Elsivera Mockery,' Aspio was shouting. 'You have foolishly allowed people to slide into the computer world and to play dangerous games there. But you forgot that when people can get in, other people can get out. People like me! Now, do you want to be sliced with the laser sword, zooted with the zoot gun, or given the elbow torture?'

And now, behind him, aliens of all kinds were oozing out of the realer-than-real pod . . . a giant slug, a small sludge dragon, eagle men, wolf women and serpents with wings. They screamed and snarled as they wriggled out of the realer-than-real and into the ordinary world.

'Our hour has struck!' Aspio shouted, raising his laser sword, just as if he intended to behead Elsivera then and there. But at that moment –

CHAPTER 29

Formby had had enough. He knew he must act
quickly before his villain turned into a total artist –
or even a hero – and before Count Aspio did something so violent that Miss Rogers would not let the
story into the school library. Not only that, Squidgy
Moot and Professor Mockery had been falling for
ages. It was time they landed. And Squidgy Moot
had particularly asked that he should not fall into
a bed. At that very moment, just when he needed
it, Formby had a good idea.

CHAPTER 30

But at that moment (he typed in, his fingers dancing across the keyboard, skilfully stealing the story away from Minnie once more) *something fell – CRUNCH – right on top of Aspio.*

CRUNCH again!

'Hey whacko!' moaned a faint voice.

Aspio had been struck by two CRUNCHES, one after the other. The first was Professor Mockery, closely followed by the second – Squidgy Moot.

Aspio had not expected attack from above. It bowled him flat on his back. His laser gun spun away while Elsivera rolled to safety once more. Aspio writhed in agony.

'Get them!' he gurgled faintly to his alien hordes, who were still slithering and sliming out of the realer-than-real pod.

They attacked at once. Battle was joined. Elsivera was just scrambling to her feet when — squelch! The giant slug flopped upon her, wrapping itself around her arms and legs. Meanwhile the small sludge dragon sank its fangs into Nina's left zoot boot. She could not kick herself free, and she could not twist her right foot to a good shooting angle, so she was forced to hop around looking absolutely ridiculous. As for Aspio, he recovered with great, alien speed. Foaming with fury he made at once for Professor Waldo, who was staggering in circles, utterly confused. Imagine Professor Waldo's feelings when he found himself confronted by a ferocious alien — an alien he actually recognized.

'Get away!' Professor Waldo yelled at them. 'You're nothing but ghosts . . . mere sketches drawn to entertain a little sister.'

'There's nothing "mere" about art,' snarled Aspio. 'You drew us and here we are — realer-than-real.'

But Squidgy Moot grabbed both the 'Eeezi-squeeze' sauce bottle and the big salt cellar from Professor Elsivera's desk. Squeedle! Schloop! He tossed salt all over the giant slug, which immediately released Elsivera, squirming and roaring as it did so, for it could not bear salt. And at the same time, Squidgy Moot was squirting tomato sauce into one of Aspio's bright-red eyes.

CHAPTER 31

'Tomato sauce!' yelled Squidgy Moot. 'Have a
heart, Formby! A villain like me can't fight with
tomato sauce. How about a laser sword, or zoot
boots like Nina's? Please! Please! I beg you! Anything but tomato sauce!'

'No!' yelled Formby. 'Look! Look!'

Words ran like maddened beetles across the
screen . . . Minnie's words, squirming through the
Internet and finding their way into the story.

CHAPTER 32

But now the wonderful Nina leaped into battle. She gave a kick so powerful that the sludge dragon went flying across the room, and then, spinning around, began firing off a further series of zoot kicks.

She also snatched up the loaf of French bread from Professor Elsivera's desk, and, quick as a minnow, she struck the sludge dragon at the back of his knees. That bread stick was extremely stale; it was as hard as a club. And it was also covered with various greenish moulds, for it had been lying around Elsivera's desk for days. The moulds exploded softly, filling the air with greenish powder. The effect was sensational.

All the aliens began gasping and staggering, for once out of the realer-than-real world they were all allergic to mouldy bread, and probably to pollen as well. Every one of them was struck down by hay fever and, since none of them had handkerchiefs, they all began dripping and sneezing convulvulously.

CHAPTER 33

'Convulvulously! Ha!' yelled Squidgy Moot. 'What sort of word is that? She means "convulsively".'

'Minnie's only eight,' said Formby, surprised to find himself sticking up for a little sister. 'Be fair! It's a pretty good idea for someone of eight. I mean, four people could easily beat a whole army if the army got hay fever and began sneezing. And "convulvulously" sounds great to me.'

'Hey!' cried Squidgy. 'Are you siding with little sisters? Is Aspio going to be beaten by mere mouldy *bread*? And is he sneezing too?'

'I'll soon fix Aspio,' said Formby. 'Watch me!'

CHAPTER 34

It is true little sisters were being quite useful (Formby typed in quickly), *but they were also trying to keep clear of Aspio who was hysterical with fury. Villains with horns hate it when something tumbles on them out of the sky. And a running nose ruins their fiendish glory. Stretching out his rubbery arm, all swollen with veins and muscles, he grabbed Professor Waldo and tossed him twenty feet into the air.*

'Oh, my poor brother!' Professor Elsivera screamed, leaping at Aspio, who merely snarled and sneezed and snatched her too, tossing her up after her brother who was on the way down by now. There

stood Aspio, evil and triumphant, gnashing his tusks (in between sneezing) while lightly juggling two university professors, one of them a Nobel Prize-winner, as if they were paper puppets.

'Now, I am going to be really nasty!' he roared as they revolved through the air. 'I'll juggle you and joggle you, then whittle you to wisps so that you'll be borne away by the westerly wind. Atchooo!'

Nina Moot fired her zoot boots at Aspio, but he simply laughed at her zoot stream.

'Ha! Ha!' he yelled. 'You have been too clever, smarty-pants! Hay fever makes aliens like me imperviable to the zoot stream.'

CHAPTER 35

'Imperviable!' shouted Squidgy. 'What sort of word is that? Let *me* at him! I'll zoot him with words.'

And, taking Formby in an unexpected hammerlock, he twitched him out of the whirl-around chair.

'My turn!' Squidgy Moot shouted, whirling himself in front of the screen, and dominating the computer keyboard.

CHAPTER 36

Swish! Clash! Zing! Slash! Squidgy Moot snatched up Count Aspio's sword from under the realer-than-real pod where it had been blown by the tempest of alien sneezes. Aspio saw him coming and, in between juggling the two professors, he actually managed to fire his evil fingernails at Squidgy, who ducked and leaped wildly, avoiding every nail.

But at this point words began racing like beetles across the screen. The little sisters had taken over again.

CHAPTER 37

But as Squidgy leaped and ducked, avoiding the fingernail darts, he stepped back on to the slippery giant slug. Squidgy's left leg slid right and his right leg slid left. He lost his balance and fell over backwards.

'Revenge!' yelled Aspio. 'Now!' And forgetting the two professors who were still in mid-air, he rushed forward crooking his fingers into claws. Things looked bad for Waldo and Elsivera tumbling out of the air with no one to catch them. However, climbing their internut had made them quick and strong. Waldo somersaulted in mid-air, landed and braced himself skilfully. A moment later, Elsivera came to rest lightly on his shoulders.

Across the room Aspio was about to sink his claws into Squidgy Moot, but Nina, who was highly skilled at rugby, flung herself forward in a superb tackle, so it was Aspio's turn to crash to the ground.

CHAPTER 38

There was a hesitation in the flow of words. Squidgy Moot leaped to the keyboard, the light of vengeance in his eye, as he took charge of the story in less than a microsecond.

'Hang on for a moment,' interrupted Formby grabbing Squidgy Moot's arm. 'Be careful! If we have too much bloodthirsty violence in our story they won't put it in the school library.'

'But this is the place where we just *have* to have bloodthirsty violence,' said Squidgy Moot.

But Formby suddenly *knew* just how to end his story in the right way. Squidgy was shouting and trying to push him away from the computer, but

Formby showed all the determination of an author who knows how to end a tale in the right way. With an ending like the one he had in mind, his book would certainly be chosen for the school library.

CHAPTER 39

Aspio lay on the ground apparently stunned. Nina ran towards him ready to fire her zoot boots, and Elsivera snatched up a nearby broom. For a moment they circled him, prepared for trickery and attack, while the other demons hooted and wailed, all too frightened to interfere.

Then Aspio raised his head. But at the sight of his face, Nina and both Professors Mockery gasped with amazement. Could that possibly be Aspio?

What had happened to him in these last confused moments? For he was utterly transformed ... altered beyond recognition. Where were his curling horns? What had happened to his tusks? The horrible hair on his ears had turned into silky fur. His elbows had become softly rounded. He had grown elegant whiskers and his evil eyes had become mild and surprised.

'Where am I? Who am I?' he asked in a new, gentle voice.

'What are you?' cried a chorus of voices, for Nina and both professors were absolutely bewildered too.

'I have saved you all,' cried a solemn voice from somewhere beyond them. Everyone swung round. There stood Squidgy Moot, triumphantly waving the bottle of 'Eezi-squeeze' tomato sauce. He was posing in front of the first drawing of Aspio that had ever been drawn ... the very same drawing that Professor Waldo had drawn for his little sister all those years ago when they were orphans in the house of their neglectful uncle. But the picture had been changed. Squidgy had altered it. By firing tomato sauce at it with the deadly accuracy of a true artist, he had changed Aspio from a horned demon, raging out of the realer-than-real, to a sweet pussycat man from the planet Purr-Purr.

'What's going on?' asked this bewildered stranger in a soft rumbling voice.

'You have just been saved!' cried Squidgy Moot. 'By me! There is no doubt about it. During the course of this story I have turned from a villain into an artist. So, in a way, I have saved myself too. Saved myself from being a villain. Saved myself through something that could make me even more money than wickedness. And now I have saved you too. We have both been saved. Saved by art.'

CHAPTER 40

Formby fell back against the back of the whirl-around chair, totally worn out.

'Hey whacko!' yelled Squidgy Moot. 'Quickly! Seal the story off while it is in a state of perfection.'

'How?' gasped Formby.

'Two words is all it needs,' said Squidgy. 'Then no little sisters will be able to ruin things by adding bits on.'

'Arrrgh! They're at it already,' gasped Formby.

But Minnie, on the computer at the public library, had only two words to add to the story, and even Formby had to admit they were the right words . . . exactly right.

CHAPTER 41

THE END

CHAPTER 42

'Those were the very words *I* had in mind,' said Squidgy Moot in amazement. 'There are times when little sisters aren't so bad after all. It must be because they copy their big brothers.'

But Formby was not so sure.

CHAPTER 43

A week later there was an assembly for the whole school. The pupils were all lined up in fairly straight lines. The teachers filed into the assembly hall, all looking keen and active, for they had all had many cups of coffee to strengthen them for the ordeal ahead.

The school band played a stirring march.

Mr Hornblower, the school principal, raised his hand and everyone fell silent, except for a soft rattling roll on the school drum. Mr Hornblower, looking a little shy, lifted his trombone from the silk-lined box beside the school microphone and blew a rather jazzy fanfare on it.

'Listen everyone!' he said. 'I have an important announcement. As you know we have been conducting a book-writing project in various classes so that our dear library will have many new books, even though we can't afford to buy any. Never forget that we are *all* storytellers at heart. And never forget that, though we may tame some stories a little by putting them into books, there are other wild tales out in the world, snapping and showing their claws, along with tales so shy we catch just a glimpse of their dappled hides as they slither off through the forest, blending into the leaves.'

'No poetry from principals,' muttered Formby Mackinaw. Miss Rogers heard him, but, for once, she did not frown at him.

'The Hornblower Book Prize has been won not by one author but by two,' Mr Hornblower went on. 'And we have an unexpected illustrator to thank too.' He paused and glanced over at Aspen Twinkler who was easy to see because he was taller than anyone else in his line.

Mr Hornblower's eyes rolled rather uneasily, before he went on with his official flattery. 'Thanks to the wonder of modern computers and desktop publishing we now have several copies of the book, and it has been bound in green and gold by Miss Rogers, who goes to bookbinding classes at the Adult Education Centre every Thursday evening. I have much pleasure in announcing that the winners of the Hornblower Book Prize are Formby and Minnie Mackinaw for their wonderful book *Saved by Art*. What a title! That's exactly the sort of title we like to see in a school library.'

There was a gasp of jealous admiration from every goody-goody in the school.

'What's the prize?' cried Formby, thrilled at the thought that he had won something for the first time in his life.

'The prize is the great honour of actually winning the prize,' said Mr Hornblower, giving Formby a severe look. 'We did think of giving you and Minnie – along with Aspen Twinkler, the illustrator – a gold medal each, but school budgets are very shaky these days, and we may have to get the coffee machine repaired quite soon. Now, the band will play the well-known song *Jerusalem* and Minnie, Formby and Aspen will come up on to the school stage to shake my hand and receive personal bound copies of *Saved by Art*.'

Formby was joined by Minnie and Aspen Twinkler, smirking proudly but looking confused too, for this was the first time in his whole life that he had ever been praised by a teacher. As they marched towards the stage, Formby heard Miss Rogers whispering to the other teachers.

'I never would have believed Formby could write a prizewinning book. Good teaching can transform a most unlikely boy,' she was saying.

'It certainly can,' Aspen's teacher whispered back, sounding even more conceited than Miss Rogers.

'Speech! Speech!' shouted the goody-goodies. They did not really want to listen to Formby, but they knew they ought to shout 'Speech! Speech!' on an occasion like this, and they were too well-behaved not to. As for Formby, he was feeling so pleased with himself he felt he could afford to be generous. He looked out over the other pupils, all writers in their own ways (though just not as good as he was). And there, on the far side of the rugby football field, he saw a line of figures watching from the shadow of the playground tree. He could make out the two Professors Mockery – the big brother and the little sister – with their arms around each other's shoulders. And there was Squidgy Moot in his black beret, sketch pad in one hand while holding out a pencil at arm's length in the other, getting a line on the glorious scene so that he could sketch it. And there, beside him, was Nina, dancing and firing coloured rockets from the zoot spikes at the end of her boots.

'I know I deserve this great honour,' Formby said modestly, speaking to Squidgy Moot and the others, just as much as he was speaking to the assembled teachers and goody-goodies, 'but I must admit that I couldn't have written this book without Aspen Twinkler's elbows, along with his illustrations, and without Minnie, my little sister. All great authors

134

need little sisters to help them push the story along.'

As he gazed at their names in gold print on the forest-green cover, Formby felt his nose begin to run through sheer happiness (as well as a little hay fever) and he was forced to wipe it on the sleeve of his school blazer. Luckily Minnie was there to take over.

'And little sisters all need challenges in life,' she said, also gazing rapturously at the golden names. 'Without big brothers constantly jeering at us, our characters would not develop.'

'I don't expect I'll need to elbow anyone for a week,' said Aspen rolling his eyes with shyness. 'I am starting my own horror comic, and it takes a lot of work.'

The teachers leaped to their feet applauding madly; the band began to play; the characters from the book began to dance in the shadow of the playground tree. Then the teachers began running around like sheep dogs, barking and herding all pupils into the school.

Later that day, Formby and Minnie ran home together without stopping off at the video arcade. They were both anxious to show their parents the beautifully bound book with their names printed in gold on the green covers.

Mr Mackinaw had come home early from work, troubled by a severe headache, the result of watching late-night horror films on television. He and Mrs Mackinaw were having a cup of tea and watching a documentary about famous paintings, as they waited patiently for what they really wanted to see – a tale of crime and treachery in a large hospital. Naturally they were amazed by the wonderful green books and the gold printing, and Mr Mackinaw was so delighted, his headache disappeared in seconds.

'Of course my grandfather was a great reader,' he said over and over again. 'The kids must take after him.'

'Oh yeah? Tell me about it!' said Mrs Mackinaw sarcastically.

Formby glanced modestly sideways while his parents began arguing over which side of the family was the most talented. On television, an art expert in glasses was speaking very seriously.

'Of course some paints don't last as long as others,' he said. 'Some of them dry up and flake away, and then whatever has been painted on the canvas underneath shows through. The famous painter Leonardo da Vinci did a few exquisite portraits using tomato sauce, but they quickly deteriorated.'

Some strange force made Formby tear his eyes from the television and look through the picture window.

In their garden, beyond the broad beans, a strange figure had suddenly appeared. Silky cats' ears rose out of its red hair. Fine whiskers sprayed out on either side of its nose. It slowly turned its head to look back through the picture window, straight at Formby. The round eyes, peering over the whiskers, were gentle enough and yet . . . and yet, as Formby peered back, a sinister expression crept into those eyes. They narrowed wickedly. The whiskers twitched, and one or two of them fell off.

'Aspio!' hissed Formby, nudging Minnie.

A passing breeze swept a strand of red hair away over the pumpkins. On either side of the head, something seemed to be twisting its way through the red curls. Formby gasped. So did Minnie! Surely they were looking at curling horns!

'The tomato sauce is flaking away,' hissed Minnie. Though painted out by Squidgy Moot, the old Aspio was struggling into existence once more.

The telephone rang. Formby, who was nearest, answered it.

'Hey kid!' said a voice. It was Aspen Twinkler. 'Hey, when you wrote about Count Aspio being so *ugly* and having such sharp elbows you weren't thinking of *me*, were you?'

'No way!' said Formby with great sincerity, but secretly crossing the fingers of his free hand so that he could tell lies freely. Through the window he could see Count Aspio looking more and more the way he had looked in the beginning as the dried tomato sauce flaked away in the breeze.

'I reckon you were making fun of me,' cried Aspen Twinkler. 'You just wait. My elbows are nothing – *nothing* – to my knees. I'll *get* you for this.'

'If you do that I won't help you with your horror comic,' said Formby quickly. 'And I won't let you illustrate any of my other stories.'

'What other stories?' asked Aspen Twinkler.

'I'm writing a lot of other stories,' said Formby, crossing his fingers even harder. 'Think about it.' Then he hung up to give Aspen plenty of time for thinking.

'Dad, can we use your computer?' Formby shouted. Luckily the tale of the dangerous hospital was just beginning.

'Of course,' said his father, greedily fixing his eyes on a particularly villainous doctor. 'I know I can trust kids who have written a book with gold printing on the cover.'

Formby went racing off to the office, Minnie at his heels.

'How will we get in touch with Nina and Squidgy?' cried Minnie, as they ran.

'They'll be round, now Aspio's loose once more,' Formby said, as they burst into the study where the computer was, quietly and smugly, waiting for them.

'We're here already,' cried Squidgy Moot, leaping out from behind the door. 'I'm armed to the teeth. I've brought my paint brush, and an "Eezisqueeze" bottle of tomato sauce . . .'

'And I've brought my zoot boots,' said Nina bouncing beside him, and practising a few high kicks.

'I'll have first go,' yelled Minnie, sliding on to the whirl-around chair.

'No, *I'll* go first,' shouted Formby, grabbing a nearby stool. 'I'm the oldest one and, anyhow, boys know more about computers than girls.'

But then he froze, for he had had an *idea* and it was a particularly amazing one.

'No! Hang on!' he cried. 'Let's *share!*'

'I was just going to say that,' said Minnie, beaming.

So, filled with good cheer and happiness, Formby and Minnie sat down side by side in front of the computer, where an entirely new horror story was lying (wickedly) in wait for them.